D1570977

www.bacongrief.com

bacon grief

for Brooks, Colt, Jack, Ollie, Charlie, Sunny, Richard, Tina, Roni, Chase, Andrew, Maximus and for everyone else who needs it

He was a man of God. And he was a man of God.

And they were loved by their family and they loved their family, each of them, although some, as happens, struggled with understanding and acceptance along the way.

He attempted high school theatre by hobby, and he loved ice cream and sprinkles, and he liked reading and libraries and quiet but also parties and confetti and the raucous nonsense times.

He loved <u>The Lord of the Rings</u> and computer games and singing and playing piano and pickles and olives and other gross things that could be forgiven, but he did NOT like sprinkles on ice cream and, in the before times, this was thought to be an inconceivable and unforgivable flaw; but, now, now that love was to be involved, clemency was being looked into.

And there they were and that was them and they were also, of course, more complicated than that but they were also, quite simply, extremely simply, perfectly simply

in love with Jesus and in love with each other.

(And so, this shall be a fairly simple story. Here is a synopsis, for those trying to save some time. Begin. Love Jesus. Love each other. End. Well, anyway, it's sort of a little bit almost like that.)

I had a girlfriend once.
I bought her a giant, stuffed Tweety Bird (registered trademark) for Valentine's Day (registered trademark). Give Hallmark a dollar and
Cut me a break, it was sixth grade.
Anyway, she cried.
The girl actually cried.
And I thought it was a real, complete and total victory and I thought she really, completely, totally loved it like in some kind of romantic comedy when some fella makes some kind of grand gesture and the girl cries and they immediately make out and get married and such: but, turns out, it wasn't so much a victory as some kind of massive misstep.
Turns out, it's really embarrassing to receive a giant, stuffed, trademark-registered Tweety Bird.
Such a gift would make you cry.
Turns out.
Even in the sixth grade.
Even though I always and still loved and love carnival games and keep playing for larger and larger stuffed animals only to always, always walk away with nothing or a pre-dead goldfish.

Anyway, I would have been grateful to receive such a giant stuffed animal, as previously described or otherwise.
I would have made out with me.
I would have married me.
Immediately and without haste.

We broke up on February fifteen.

I had a girlfriend once.
This was to be a sordid love affair, albeit, again and obviously brief.
This time I learned. Of course.
This time, there was no stuffed animal of any kind.
Trademark or no.
This was a boring relationship. We did touch, on accident, in the school hallway.
It was gross.
And then, doing math homework over the phone, as power couples do, I said,
"Yeah, I don't think this is working."
She agreed. She said the math doesn't add up. That would be literal except, obviously we were way beyond addition. This was, like, the seventh grade or something.
"Oh, no. I'm sorry. My homework is fine."
"Well. What's the answer?"
"I meant us." We said simultaneously.
"I just think we'd probably make better friends, or something. I mean, I like you, sort of. I guess."
"Oh."
"By the way, I think the answer is four hundred seventy-three point twenty-one."
"Yeah." Sob. "That's what I got."

The other time I had a girlfriend was in the eighth grade when a girl wanted to take me horseback riding.

So, we went horseback riding.
Turns out, when a girl asks you to go horseback riding that's, like, a date, and if she asks you to go horseback riding again, then you're like, dating.
In a relationship.
Boyfriend and girlfriend.

I no longer go horseback riding.

It's not so much that I don't want to accidentally find myself in relationships as I don't like being thrown from horses.
It hurts.
But it's also nice not to accidentally find myself in relationships.

Later, as a good socialite does, I would go to all of our high school dances.
To which it would basically, more or less, be requisite to take a girl.
So I would.
Humblebrag.
Statistically, it turns out, three times out of three, that girl thinks you're super into her.
Basically, three times out of three, if you're not some kind of careful, you've got yourself a girlfriend.

One time I would wear Christmas lights to a high school dance.
It would be amazing.
My sister would pin them upon my JCPenny pin-stripe suit and there would be GIGANTIC battery packs in all of my pockets.
It would make quite an impression.

Of course, the girl taken to the immediately aforementioned dance would make me promise to marry her.

So, no, I've never really been all that good with girls.

Growing up Catholic is kind of hilarious. I'm sure you agree.

They don't tell you why you do anything. So, here's the plan. Dress up, kind of. Save your best clothing – you know, for me, that's the fancy shirt, the one with the buttons, and the bowtie, because neckties are stupid [and, did you know my story would be so quickly, so divisive? Well anyway, I submit necktie lovers can keep reading even though they're wrong (and also the bowtie is fake because ZERO human beings have time for real bowties – robots and other artificial intelligence probably do)] – for Christmas and Easter but, still, this isn't casual Friday. In here, it's not your Sunday best, per se, but leave the cargo shorts[1] at home.

(Actually, let's get this out of the way. We don't wear cargo shorts. Go, take those to your nearest donation bin. For some reason, Goodwill accepts them AND gives your parents a tax deduction letter despite the utter uselessness and total lack of resale ability.

Go ahead. We'll wait.

I assure you, this is for the best.)

[So. *Divisive.*]

---

[1] Cargo shorts were apparently invented in the 1940s for the Air Force to use in World War II. Someone else on the internet says they were worn by the British in the 1930s. I don't know WHY we need to fight over who came up with them. Instead, also according to the internet, they are hated because they look terrible on men. This, we know to be correct.

And back to Catholicism and not knowing anything about it, but we are good Catholics so we still do everything, and we always, always sit in the same pew and we genuflect (this is one of the BEST words and is too rarely used), and we sit and we stand and when the bells ring the bread turns into actual Jesus and, I think, the miracle is that it still tastes stale and weird.

We're there. Most of us don't know why we do what we do, but we do it every week, over and over again and we are there.

Until we aren't.

I fell in love with this youth group at a Baptist church down the street because it was funny and meaningful and also because they had pizza. And while it was probably the pizza, it could have also been that I actually heard a bunch of adults speaking a language about the Bible (that made sense to me) that kept me going. But, to be perfectly transparent, it was actually the pizza.

(Also, while cargo shorts are evidently, inexplicably allowed here, we still never, never wear them. When they say love the sinner, not the sin, it is my belief that this is what they may be referring to).

Now that I have been going to this small group for the past two years, I truly feel a greater understanding of Jesus and who he is and what his message actually means - much more than I ever got in fourteen years of Catholicism, which is not necessarily intended to be a knock on Catholicism. After all, it is the root of all of our denominations.

It's the root of who I am.

Indeed, Catholicism is calisthenics, but it's so much more than that. No matter what this youth group teaches me or what church I end up belonging to, I'll always go back to my family church from time to time to worship with them because it's important to them - and, frankly, it's important to me.

I just also like a greater understanding of Jesus.

And pizza. Duh.

1/ Hey. Hi! Hey.

2/ Hey! How are you? I'm just checking this chat feature out. It's pretty neat[2].

1/ We don't say neat. In fact, no one says neat.

2/ Cool[3]! I meant cool! Everyone still says cool, right?

1/ Yep. Cool.

2/ Cool.

1/ Okay, probably too much.

2/ Right. Anyway, have you been on this thingy long?

1/ Thirty-seven years.

2/ Oh. Um, I'm fourteen. So…

1/ Right.

2/ …

1/ I'm totally kidding. I don't even think the Internet is that old. And certainly not this chatroom. I think it's brand-new. Anyway, I've been on for forty-two minutes. It just feels like years and years and years. Are you really a Christian? There's so few of us on here.

---

[2] It's actually JUST fine to say neat, turns out. According to Merriam-Webster, it means free from dirt and disorder. It also means marked by skill or ingenuity. But it ALSO means very pleasant, fun, or enjoyable. In a sentence, then, we could say, this footnote is neat. Indeed.

[3] Cool means moderately cold. It also means very good or excellent, but not until the SEVENTH definition. So, I guess that's neat.

2/ Oh yeah! My faith is pretty important to me. What church do you go to around here? Oh, hey, it looks like you and I might go to the same school! That's neat.

2/ I mean, cool. It's cool.

1/ ...

2/ Did you go? Did you leave? Are you gone? Hello...

1/ ...

1/ No. I'm just pulling your leg. I'm not like that. You can say neat. You can say anything you want. I mean, almost anything. Nearly anything. Words are my jam.

2/ Yeah? What's your favorite word?

1/ Shemomedjamo[4].

2/ Uh, yeah. Okay, I've no idea. Like, my favorite word is probably spike or something. So.

1/ Shemomedjamo, I guess, kind of means I ate it all. Something like that. Anyway, I like weird words.

2/ Shemomedjamo. Cool.

1/ Why is your favorite word probably spike[5]?

---

[4] This word comes from Georgia. Not, like, the state. Someone from Atlanta did not come up with this word. It literally means, I accidentally ate the whole thing. There is no English equivalent, which is a real shame. Someone from Atlanta COULD come up with one...

[5] Shockingly, NOT one of the top 100 dog names.

2/ Oh. It isn't. I mean I like to play volleyball. Honestly I just made that up. I don't know that I have a favorite word.

1/ But do you like eating? Because I kind of like shemomedjamo because I like eating.

2/ Well, yeah. For sure. What's your favorite food?

1/ Cheese.

2/ Mmmm.

1/ Yes, I consider myself something of a turophile[6].

2/ Indeed.

1/ Oh! You know turophile!

2/ No, but I know antecedents and context clues. I'm no dummy. Example: you said your favorite food, ala the food you most love in this world, is cheese. Which, for the record, is kind of a cop out because I'm nearly certain there are at least hundreds, if not thousands, of cheeses. This guy put, like, five hundred and forty-seven kinds of cheese on a pizza and got a world record so, it's a thing. Anyway, immediately thereafter you referred to yourself as a turophile. A cheese-lover. Bam!

1/ Touché.

2/ Neat word. Er.

---

[6] See also, caseophile. For real. TWO words for lovers of cheese! Appropriate.

1/ Cool.

2/ Cool.

When he was seven years old, he first knew he wasn't heterosexual - he just didn't know the word for it. He also knew it wouldn't be an issue with his family. He was pretty sure they knew before he did; after all, his purple pants were his favorite. NOT THAT A HETEROSEXUAL WOULDN'T WEAR PURPLE PANTS. This is encouraged behavior which would likely result in greater happiness for heterosexuals. This begins and ends his presidential campaign.

On the other hand, while he also knew from a young age - though it's more difficult for him to define exactly - he knew his family of pastors and churchgoers and homeschoolers would take major issue with this unforgivable defiance, for that's what they saw this as.

His family would see it as, we just want you to be happy, after all.

His family would encourage therapy and would eventually hold paid-for college tuition as endangered remuneration.

Two perspectives. Maybe not a right way to look at it. Maybe, maybe not, a wrong way to look at it.

Either way, it turns out, the Lord is in the details.

The devil isn't.

1/ There is a three-pronged test.

2/ What does that even mean? Also, you should know, I have mild test anxiety. So, it is possible that any failure would be outside of my control.

1/ Nope. Hear me out. This is very simple. It's only if you meet or exceed any of these three fine criteria, that you're more than likely beyond repair.

One - do you wear, or would you wear (should you be so blessed as to have every resource available) purple pants?

2/ No.

1/ Oh. Well, that's rude.

2/ No, I mean I like yours. Yours are fine. Yours look great. On you.

Only, I just wonder if you maybe shouldn't wear them QUITE so often.

1/ Okay, okay, so all I heard was that purple pants are great, specifically my purple pants are great, and that definitely counts. I mean it's still ridiculous for you not to concern yourself with how good you would look in such an iconic piece of fashion for our times, but this is not a complete disaster. Yet.

Two - would you ever, ever, anywhere, ever be seen in cargo pants?

2/ I mean it's just really, really nice to have all of those pockets at one's disposal.

1/ OHMYGOSHWEARAFANNYPACK[7]. Seriously. I think they're coming back.

2/ I can see where you are going with this, and while I wish greatly that fanny packs were coming back, I think you might be ahead of your time. I can agree that cargo pants are not the most flattering.

1/ ACCEPTABLE ANSWER. Finally, and most importantly, do you think I'm insanely attractive?

2/ In purple pants?

1/ NO. Well, yes, although that is obvious. I mean in general. With and without pants. PURPLE. Oh my gosh I am the MOST sorry. The sorriest. I meant in any pants, or not in any pants, irrespective of color. Pants or no pants. I'm sorry. Typing doesn't seem to be going particularly well for me right now and I should...

2/ Stop talking. Yes, you're attractive. The most attractive. In pants of all colors.

1/ Well. Congratulations, good sir. You've passed the test.

Wait.

You passed with, I would say, a B+. But, that's more than admirable. We struggled with the pockets a little.

2/ Right, but you have yet to tell me what I was being tested on?

---

[7] In the 1950s, in Britain, the fanny pack was referred to as the bum bag. This is unfortunate. Nevertheless, a 5,000-year-old mummy was discovered in 1991 with a fanny pack. That's right, WAY before Jesus.

1/ Oh. You're definitely gay. And so we can be in a relationship, I mean, if you want to. And also, you should really, really, definitely probably soon, actually talk to your parents.

Also, I'm Charlie.

"TIMOTH!"

That's short for Timothy. And it's not exactly screamed, per se, not precisely an exclamation of fear or anger so much as some kind of very, very stern annoyance.

I'm in the car with him and his mother, Mrs. Timoth. I assume she has a first name but, as of this moment, we've all only just met so, that remains unconfirmed.

"Hahahah hahahahaha. Guffaw. Hahaha hahaha. Etc."

That's him laughing at me. Not his mother.

"What's wrong with you two?"

"I'm sorry, Mrs. T, it's just."

"You know? In my day, we respected our elders. That's what we did. We didn't speak unless we were spoken to. We minded. That's what we did."

And she, this woman, she's just exactly what you think she is. The mother of thirty-seven, homeschool teacher, pastor's wife, type. I mean, I have no idea how many children she has. Thirty-seven, thirty-eight[8], the point remains the same. Timothy's mom is the mom you need when you need homemade pie. That could be insulting. I don't know. I'm probably just hungry.

"I'm sorry. You're so very right. It's just? In this instance, well, sometimes there is a situation that may befit..."

---

[8] Six. She has six kids.

"Honestly."

"What? I'm trying to..."

"Ma. He's an idiot. A loveable, CERTAINLY apologetic, buffoon. A real horse's..."

"LANGUAGE!"

"I said horse. In the possessive but, still. Horse."

The thing is, this is an emergency and I'm in some kind of pain and Timothy knows this because he seems to somehow know more and more about me and he is clearly and very, very thoroughly enjoying himself.

"Mrs. Timothy's mom, would it be possible that I...?"

"It's these bridges. They build them with two lanes, that's what they did. Far too much traffic and there's no other way around. We need more lanes."

"Right, so, just as soon as..."

"I think we're going to be late. I don't like being late to church. We are never late to church. Your father. If there was just another lane. It wouldn't take too much construction. Lord knows we're used to it. Pylon season, that's what it is. [9]"

"Ma, we go to church four times a week. We are late about three point seven eighths of those times."

---

[9] I suppose the traffic is a bit heavy. But I would argue against construction. It's widely considered that Illinois has four seasons. I don't remember the joke but, something like, construction, more construction, blah blah, basically the pylons are permanent. So are the potholes.

"Auxiliary Services. Never Sunday. Not on the Lord's day. On time, this family.[10]"

"OK. I, for one, super, absolutely, one-hundred percent believe in your timeliness. It's just, I'm in serious need of."

"Timothy. Is something wrong with your friend? It looks very much like something is wrong with your friend."

"That's what I was…"

"His name's Charles, mom. You've met a time or two. Or seven. I know we're new here."

"He's nervous. That's what he is. Do you go to church, son?"

"LISTEN I JUST REALLY NEED TO…"

"His name is Charles, not son, and he does go to church, Ma. We've discussed all of this. Had the Jesus conversation, remember, that's how we met?"

"OK, so I'm having a lovely time chatting with both of you, but if you don't mind, I'd love to…"

---

[10] We're already three minutes late.

The thing is, I think last night I ate too much pepperoni pizza or maybe drank too much Coca Cola or possibly it was the big Nerds. You know those? Sour nerds, regular nerds, gummy nerds, tropical nerds? Variations on variations, all of them fantastic, but they really outdid themselves on the big, chewy ones. I could eat boxes and boxes. See last night for example.

"I say he's just nervous, poor fella. Going to a new church can do that. Hey, thank you for tagging along. You're going to love it. If we ever get there. We're such a good bunch."

Timothy does his best impression of his mother here and, to be honest, it's decent: "Yeah, kiddo, and if you're good, maybe we'll get *pizza* after."

And he knows. I know he knows. I can tell he knows, and I hate him, I like him but I hate him.

"Mrs. Mother of Timoth, I know we are running behind but..."

"BUTT."

I hate him. I don't even like him. I hate him.

"I hate you."

"You know your dad has a special sermon today about the taming of the tongue. I think you'll both benefit from it, that's what I..."

"LISTEN IF I DON'T TAKE A RATHER MASSIVE DUMP IN THE NEXT TWENTY-THREE SECONDS, I'M AFRAID OF WHAT MIGHT HAPPEN TO MY CLOTHING AND THIS OTHERWISE LOVELY VEHICLE."

That's when I realize we are in the car and we are in the parking lot and it's June and the windows are down and about forty-seven[11] people are also late, it seems.

And I run inside.

---

[11] Eleven. There are eleven people in the parking lot.

You can tell a church is fancy by the automatic flushing, which, if you think about it, really think about it, is a sort of misguided luxury.

Hear me out.

I step into this stall and, obviously, I really have to take a seat immediately and yet, to my right, above the gleaming, gold-laden toilet paper dispenser [it's actually just a regular toilet paper dispenser, but I wanted to exaggerate in an effort to establish the extravagance of my surroundings – I mean, here, the stall door actually latches (!)] is a large, flat box of tissue paper, clearly labelled toilet seat covers[12][13], and this is something that we just don't have at the Catholic church, and I feel confused but also, somehow, obligated, and who honestly has *time* for this?

Apparently, I do.

Miracle of miracles.

Anyway, I'm just here trying to make a good first impression and already blowing it – there are better word choices – so I decide to follow the protocol and remove one of these tissues which are folded in half and, when unopened, take on the shape and size of a toilet seat. So, that's a clever schematic.

---

[12] The toilet seat cover was invented in 1942 by JC Thomasa. You can see an original at a museum in Texas. To save you some time, it looks roughly the same as the one in a stall near you. Someone invented a coin-operated version. Someone else invented an automatic, self-renewing toilet seat cover. For real! Look it up. It's, um, just, ew?

[13] Thanks, Wikipedia. Seriously, if everyone could just donate $3....

There are lines here, cut out, not all the way around but, sort of, perforated and it looks like you're supposed to take out the middle, and I'm trying not to dilly-dally so I just, sort of, rip at it and eventually my piece of tissue paper further unfolds to appear something like a misshapen donut with the middle of the inside hanging on to the back of the outside[14].

So that's fine, this must be how it goes. So, I put it on the toilet seat, just so, with the middle part sort of dangling into the water, and I go to sit down, and, I guess it's the amount of shifting around I must have done when trying to complete my lavatory origami, or the sensor malfunctions, or perhaps I turned just out of view, because the toilet flushes. And it's loud and sort of splashy, but it's clean water, so I'm not super offended, and I turn around in time to watch it suck the cover away and here we are, and I didn't even WANT the stupid thing but now, you and me toilet, well, I feel obligated, and furthermore, I feel challenged by you, and one thing I know is that I'm going to win.

I pull out another toilet seat cover. I rip at the thing again, with the middle dangling as before and I turn around really fast and go to sit down as fast as I can and sure enough it flushes again and it splashes again and this time I feel the bare seat underneath me and the cold wet is unexpected and gross but it's still, ultimately, clean water and okay, fine, let's try to live into this luxurious offering just one more time.

---

[14] For the record, to this day, there is much debate over the orientation of the flappy doohickey in the middle of the disposable covers. Something about preventing splashing. I don't buy it.

After all, there's a rule of three in life, so this will work. It has to. And also, I still really, really have to go to the bathroom, so far be it from me to continue to disobey my bowels because they're going to win out sooner or later.

This time I completely tear out the middle and throw it into the toilet ahead of time. After all, it says they're flushable and the thing has already proven itself twice, and also, I'm wasting a lot of water here.

Naturally, third time's a charm and my seat is successful and more or less dry, and the rest of the movement is grand indeed.

You know, I really could get used to toilet seat covers. To this particular brand of luxury.

I've yet to buy into the automatic flush, however.

Tim's dad's sermon was really, remarkably, decent. Not that I should have expected less. I mean, it wasn't on anything controversial, unless controlling speech, at least in public, is controversial. I don't know. We all say things we're not proud of, I suppose. I guess Mrs. Tim was super unimpressed by my rather public outburst in the car, as an example.

Anyway, I'm the first to admit how very far I am from perfect.

But, I didn't fall asleep so that's a sign of an engaging homily! Rather, sermon. Granted, I was trying to make a good first impression with his family, so I really tried hard NOT to fall asleep.

Okay, the point is, I missed about twenty minutes of it from my hardships in the gold-laden facilities, but overall, church was quite pleasant today.

Of course, it's a small church and everyone knows everyone; so, at the end of it all, people were coming up to the pastor's family and, specifically, to Tim and oh, "Who's your friend"[15] and "is he new to town" and "has he seen the bathrooms here," and on and on, and he introduces me to several people and I smile and nod; and, finally, someone addresses me directly and she's, maybe, seventy-three years old; I'm just guessing.

"What brings you here today, son?"

"Oh, well, I'm with Tim."

---

[15] The people who overheard my declaration in the parking lot, notably, do NOT offer introductory remarks.

It's probably ill-advised to say you're *with* someone. Just something I'm learning along the way.

"He's just checking out the church, Francine." Tim jumps in as an attempt to save the day.

"Oh yes, Tim just *loves* this guy, don't you Tim?"

Tim's mother is attempting to help in the most non-helpful way.

"Uh, that's right. Tim's a very good dude."

And, I think "good dude[16]" really works here. It's very convincing. Meanwhile, nerves abound, and I just want out of this situation.

"I see," and this super-judgy human is looking at me like she knows about all the wasted water. Anyway, she says, "well, I'm glad to see Tim is making *friends* so quickly, here." And she says, "I guess I'll see you at lunch."

Lunch? I mean, I am hungry now...

---

[16] See also, "buddy" and "pal" as acceptable nomenclature.

He was a good Catholic boy growing up in central Illinois.

And he was a Southern Baptist in Tennessee.

He had a guinea pig[17] and a parakeet[18] and a couple of lizards[19] - the little green ones that lose their tails and regrow them - NATURALLY AND WITHOUT ANY SORT OF OWNER INTERVENTION OF COURSE - and a bunny rabbit[20] and a tree frog[21] but never a cat nor a dog and never all of these things at once. This wasn't a zoo, after all. This was his portion of a small, three-bedroom apartment. Sensible.

And he loved the outdoors and spent as much time as he could climbing trees and wading in the river. He also had many pets but just by claiming them as he found them and leaving them in the wilderness and, he swears, he would live in a tent if he could and would often ask his mother if that was an option, to which, depending on the level of tomfoolery, she might be tempted to offer an affirmative reply.

And so, they both grew up in the church, states away from each other, and it was always a part of their lives. And each of them took to it more and more seriously as their childhoods progressed.

---

[17] Cody.

[18] Pepper.

[19] Peanut Butter and Jelly.

[20] Barbra.

[21] Federico Ferdinand Francisco the Fourth. He was NOT the fourth frog. I will not be known as a serial frog killer. I've just always adored alliteration.

He accepted Christ as a freshman in high school and had very recently started going to a youth group and would eventually leave Catholicism for a Baptist Church, where they would first meet in person.

He would relocate from Tennessee with his family and his dad, naturally, would serve as a pastor at a Baptist Church in central Illinois.

Indeed, they would inevitably meet, and they would instantly connect. In some kind of way.

But this wasn't falling in love. Not yet.

Tim didn't tell me about the lunch. Of course, he didn't. One, I think you're just supposed to know these things. Like, I think people in certain church traditions go to a before-church social hour followed by church - which may or may not be multiple hours long and may or may not include a snack break at intermission - followed by luncheon, followed by Sunday school or something in some sort of order that, more or less, equates to more hours than an average school day. On top of that, Tim has to maintain variations on this schedule multiple times a week.

My family, we go to the already-condensed Saturday night service, and if we leave before communion, we have enough time to binge two or even three episodes of whatever medical documentary my dad deems appropriate for dinner. Seriously, he thinks it's hilarious how much my mom abhors this weekly practice. I have to be honest with you, he's usually correct; it's often, at minimum, humor-adjacent.

At lunch, Francine, she's introducing me to everyone. To all of the twenty-six people that stuck around, I counted, she's saying this is Tim's *friend*. You know, how people say *friend* when they mean, I don't know, whatever they mean that *isn't* friend.

She's old, but she really feels like she's caught onto something and she's reveling in it.

And she has. Obviously. Luckily, everyone seems engrossed in their chicken. And me, I'm thinking how funny it would be if last night's extremely-detailed documentary on the tragically-botched and bloody hip replacement – poor guy – was just projected onto the wall right here and now[22].

But the fact that Francine just feels like she's privileged to be in on some kind of joke is making me uncomfortable.

And the fact that I, of course, have nothing to hide. That I, of course, have the same right to be here as she does. The fact that I, of course, really enjoyed the part where the surgeon found metal sludge inside the patient upon reopening the poor guy[23].

The chicken tastes the same.

"Francine, I just really appreciate how it feels like you've rolled out the red carpet for me. Do you all not get visitors very often?"

"Oh no, sweetie. Not very many *like you*. I'm just thrilled to see you here. You know what they say. You can really tell who someone is by who their friends are and all."

Of course, I know what that means.

"I don't know what that means, Francine."

---

[22] Educational programming during mealtimes can be a very effective method of increasing productivity and retention. That's what dad tells mom, anyway.

[23] Seriously. It's weird and it's on Netflix. Use your bookmark. I'll wait.

"I'll be praying for you, dearie.[24]"

---

[24] See also, "honey," "sweetie," "darling," and other words for "If you could feel as uncomfortable as possible, please, that would be just great, thanks. Be a doll and pass the salt?"

TIM/ Yeah, so, sorry about yesterday.

CHARLIE/ Why? No, yesterday was really fun. Church was great. Nothing to be sorry about. Well, that old woman. You can be sorry about her if you want?

TIM/ Francine. Yeah, she's pretty precious.

CHARLIE/ I mean, that's a word. There are others that could be used. Such as, intense, strange, a busy-body, gossip, pick-a-little[25] lady, etc.

TIM/ I'm sorry? Pick-a-little lady?

CHARLIE/ It's a musical theatre reference. Are you not familiar with the canon of musical theatre?

TIM/ Cannon? Like a big gun that plays the music whilst shooting out tap dancers and opera singers and the like?

CHARLIE/ Yes. EXACTLY that. Anyway, a pick-a-little lady is from THE MUSIC MAN, which is the musicale in which we performed last year. I was an anvil salesman. I actually had to kiss the leading female. I'll have you know I was VERY convincing[26].

TIM/ Is there video of this? There MUST be video of this.

---

[25] "Pick a little, talk a little, pick a little, talk a little, cheep, cheep, cheep, talk a lot, pick a little more." These are the genius, Tony-award winning lyrics of a 1950s classic.

[26] I wasn't.

CHARLIE/ I hope not. Also, the anvil salesman's ACTUAL name is Charlie which, I'm pretty sure, is how I got cast.

TIM/ Well, I sure hope you lived up to your name. Making out with women though…how does this fit in with your ARE YOU GAY test or whatever that was?

CHARLIE/ Oh, I just said I was convincing[27]. BY NO MEANS did I say I enjoyed it. She was a senior female though, so it was great for my street cred.

TIM/ Okedoke, but you just ACTUALLY said both musicale and street cred in the same chat, so.

---

[27] I wasn't.

33

They were innocent, once.

They always are. Once upon a time.

They were the type that skipped rocks and made Mancala out of egg cartons. The type that collected stamps and traded Pokémon cards.

Something happens.

It always does.

And when it does, afterwards, every day, he prays for it to go away. Without ceasing, he prays, Lord, heal me. Take away my sin. Make me just like everyone else.

He prays a similar prayer at first. He prays to be acceptable to God, he prays that He take away his desire, he regularly prays that. He just asks that he is able to maintain his keen fashion sense.

And so they pray. And in that way they're exactly the same. Or, they were.

He still does. He prays for forgiveness for his thoughts and for a change to his nature and a ceasing of actions that seem inevitable.

He listens, on the other hand. He sits and waits now. And every once in a while, if he's really patient and he really listens, he feels like he can hear something. He feels like he hears almost a sort of reassurance. He feels like his requests have been heard for years and he begins to understand that, maybe, just maybe, nothing has changed because nothing is wrong.

On a good day, he hears,

I accept you just the way you are.

He hears,

I always have.

And he hears,

I always will.

CHARLIE/ Do you know what we need?

TIM/ Good grades. A college education. A promising career.

CHARLIE/ Well, I guess, yes, all of that. But also, try again.

TIM/ We need a home and a dog and a van and children?

CHARLIE/ Whoa. I can support a dog, you know, IN THE VERY DISTANT FUTURE. Honestly, what is wrong with you? All of this talk of years and years, decades and centuries down the road. Right now, today, this instant, do you know what we need?

TIM/ AN ALL-DISNEY SINGALONG[28]!!!!!!

CHARLIE/ No. Ew. This is probably why your family forbids you to watch movies, though. For that, I applaud them.

TIM/ Okay okay fine, I give up. What do we need?

CHARLIE/ Obviously, the answer is ice cream. Listen, I know we're just getting to know each other. All of that. But regarding a love for regular ice cream consumption, I have been perfectly transparent.

---

[28] Honestly, the author that lives in the footnotes is for this. Charlie's go-to Disney sing-a-long song would be "Kiss the Girl," obviously. Tim will sing "Poor Unfortunate Souls" or, perhaps, "Just Around the Riverbend" because, why not?

TIM/ Touché.

CHARLIE/ I LOVE THAT WORD. Anyway, let's go get ice cream. Say yes? Oh, and tell your parents all of our friends are coming. We can send group selfies. Is a selfie of a group still a selfie?

TIM/ Groupie?

CHARLIE/ That's very dumb.

TIM/ Yes.

"No." Tim's mom and dad declare in simulcast.

"Just like that?" He responds, though he was prepared for the answer. After all, this is how it's always been.

"Yes, I'm sorry, but I don't think it's a good idea," she says.

"Can you tell me why it isn't a good idea? I mean, ALL of our friends are going."

"You don't always get a reason." Tim's dad, this time.

Tim sighs. "Okay, that's very parental and hardly makes sense."

"You're just not going. We are still in charge here and you're not going." More from Tim's dad.

"Right. But why not, again?"

"Son, we care about you. We like this kid, this friend of yours, Charles is it? He seems like a really grand fellow and we are glad you're both hanging out at youth group and going to church. We just think you're spending too much time together, maybe. I mean, given what our family has been through. Given that part of the reason we moved was to give you a fresh start. There just have to be rules. We know you mean well, but we've been down this road once and we can't move every time. You just have to be so careful," Tim's dad offers.

"You do realize this is a group of people going to get some ice cream, right? I mean this isn't, like, a sex convention or whatever."

"Son, we definitely, *definitely* don't talk like that in this household."

"Yes, I know. And we don't dance in this household and we don't go to the movie theatre or even watch movies in this household, and we don't believe in Mickey Mouse[29] or Santa Claus[30]. We do still eat ice cream in this household, right?" Tim says.

"Well, it's a lot of sugar. That's what it is." Tim's mom offers an attempt at humor to lighten the mood.

Tim plays along. "Mom, they have this low-sugar stuff now. I mean it's absolute trash, but you know me, I'm all about compromise."

"Okay, then who else is going?"

"Oh, don't worry. Some women. Lots and lots of women. So many women, it's basically the safest of safe zones."

"You're being ridiculous," she replies.

"I'm being ridiculous. Dad said 'grand fellow'. Also, THIS IS ICE CREAM. And we've already conceded to the low-sugar varieties."

"You can go. One condition," his dad says.

---

[29] Mickey was originally going to be named Mortimer. He was the first cartoon character to ever speak. In other words, he is IMPORTANT and he MATTERS and we support him.

[30] Washington Irving, the author that gave us the headless horseman, is credited for coming up with Santa's chimney entrance in a short story called *Knickerbocker's History of New York*.

Tim's eyes widen with excitement. He tries to stifle and says, "What now? Okay, I'll only consume water. I'll get a sno cone with no flavoring. Or, I'll get ice cream just like everyone else, but I'll only look at it. Maybe I'll stir it up with the spoon and watch it melt, but then I'll throw it away. Fair?"

"You have to schedule your next therapy appointment."

Therapy is for the birds.

But he goes.

He goes because he is told to go and, in general, he really does try to do what he's told to do.

He's a good boy. A good son. A good brother. A good friend. A good Christian. A good person.

He's good.

He's healthy. Well rounded. Intelligent. A decent driver, so far.

A terrible tennis player. A mediocre public speaker. A horrible dancer, not that he knows. Of course not. Not in his household.

But otherwise.

He's good.

Except he's gay.

Only he's not, of course he's not, of course this is a phase, of course this is a sinful lifestyle choice and, of course this is all just FOR A LIMITED TIME ONLY.

Of course, that's why he needs the therapy[31].

---

[31] Illinois was the fifth state to ban conversion therapy for minors, doing so in 2015. It's yet to banned in Tennessee and thirty other states. Christian counseling for all ages is widely available.

TIM/ He asked me how I planned to have a family!

CHARLIE/ What?

TIM/ YES. He said, son, THE THERAPY GUY CALLS ME SON, he said, son, if having a family is a goal of yours, as if having a family is a goal of mine and, I don't know, maybe it is, maybe it isn't, anyway, he said, don't you feel like, ultimately, you'd need a wife to make that happen?

CHARLIE/ Honestly how out of touch is this human being? First of all, I do encourage you to think of a dog[32] as the only family you and yours might eventually need but, assuming you really DO think children are cute – to which I agree, from a distance, adorbs – there are infinite opportunities for that to occur.

TIM/ Precisely! So I said, essentially that, you'll be pleased to know I've been listening to you so I definitely led off with dogs and animals being children and all of that precious nonsense. GUESS what he said, regarding the human progeny, as it were.

CHARLIE/ Progeny?

TIM/ Go with it.

CHARLIE/ Okay okay okay. Progeny. Cool. He said, those children wouldn't ACTUALLY be yours?

TIM/ Yes! He said you can't have children the natural way. God's way. Therefore, you can't fulfill your natural purpose. Something like that.

---

[32] My dog is named Maximus. I long to have a tiny dog alongside him, obviously, named Minimus.

CHARLIE/ So all we're meant to do is have children?

TIM/ Progeny.

CHARLIE/ Your parents hired this guy. They must think he's right. I mean, obviously. Do they say anything about fostering, adoption, and other honorable activities of the sort?

TIM/ They're largely silent on the subject.

CHARLIE/ Of course. My mom AND my dad, both, had eight siblings. Solid Catholic families. Lots and lots of progeny there.

TIM/ In other words, your grandparents fulfilled their purpose many, many times.

CHARLIE/ It feels like that could be read inappropriately. In fact, I feel very, very dirty right now.

TIM/ Yeah, me too. You're probably right. We aren't meant to think of these things. Definitely, definitely not.

CHARLIE/ Let's go back and delete all of this later[33].

---

[33] As you can see, we did not.

While I was Catholic, my neighbors were Baptist, and they were having more fun than I was or it seemed like they were having more fun than I was and, anyway, Catholicism was made of all of this great mystery and the aforementioned calisthenics that I didn't understand and their level of fun made me jealous, so of course I accepted their invitation to tag along.

I mean it was week after week of paintball and bowling and ice cream and swimming and video games. And pizza. There was always a level of pizza I appreciated but never fully understood. The first time I stood in line with my dollar, because that's what I was told it cost, a dollar, I just remember receiving approximately forty-seven slices of pizza. Tiny squares of pizza, thin crust, in other words, the greatest type of pizza[34]. I think in the real world the value of pizza I received was more like, I don't know, thirteen dollars, but maybe guests get a twelve-dollar coupon or maybe this is just the type of charity the Baptists around here dole out and, if so, I obviously approve.

Anyway, inevitably, eventually they paid a visit to my house.

Not my neighbors. They were at my house with some frequency. This was a visit from my new church friends.

---

[34] This is indisputable. In a study that I'm currently writing in which I speak with great authority, tiny, thin squares of pizza are proven to be the best kind of pizza, hands down. In fact, thin, tiny squares of pizza narrowly beat those adorable pizza bagel bite thingies, which are also, studies show, delightful. The dissimilarity of bagel bites to actual pizza officially disqualifies them from the study, thus leaving tiny, thin squares of pizza the clear frontrunner. Absolutely disqualified from the study are such things as cauliflower crusts and crusts that are thicker than a Texas toast sandwich, both of which are proven by the study to be abominations.

At first, it was weird, having them over, out of the blue, such as it were. But it was also exciting for some reason. The youth pastor befriended my parents and I showed my bird and my lizard and my guinea pig and my tortoise[35] to the other kids. And then I took them outside and showed them my bunny rabbits[36] and chickens[37].

Yes. I know exactly what you're thinking. All of those animals. Girl magnet. And I would ordinarily agree except only we know by now this isn't that kind of book.

Anyway, my new church friends were over for a couple of hours and they asked me all sorts of questions. They said, 'What do you know about Heaven?' And I said, I suppose I know that it's where we go when we die. And they said, 'What do you know about Hell?' And I said, I guess some people go there too?

I said it like that. Like a question instead of an answer.

They said, do you know you'll go to Heaven? I quickly said, well, yes, sure, yeah I'll go. Then they asked me why.

Why?

I don't know. Because I'm a relatively good person and I haven't killed anyone? I don't think I said that, exactly.

---

[35] Thomas.

[36] Unnamed.

[37] Simply referred to as dinner.

And I suppose it's weird to have this happen. Like it is when Jehovah's Witnesses[38] or the Church of Latter Day Saints or that guy with the miracle cleaning solution[39] knocks on your door. Only I guess this might have been a touch less weird because I knew these people, at least in theory. But my parents didn't. And we just let them in, those three years ago. We didn't question it, didn't see a reason to. I don't know about my parents, but for me, for some reason, I liked having them there. Sharing my zoo, sharing my life – parts of it, admittedly, the easier, the more marketable parts. And, again, here we are a few years later, I can't say that I remember the details of the conversation. All the answers to all the questions.

What I'll never forget, what I can't forget, what I don't ever want to forget, no matter how much I sleep.

That was the moment, that was the conversation in which I fully realized Jesus Christ as my savior.

That my relationship with Jesus was what would get me to Heaven. That, and that alone.

---

[38] No lack of love, but, for real, they don't believe in BIRTHDAYS. Has no one told them Denny's will give you an entire breakfast, like, a huge one, for ZERO DOLLARS on the date of your birth? Surely that's persuasive.

[39] Mother bought it. She swears by the stuff. Practically sells it for him. As you might expect, his visits have increased.

And, if that were true – and it is: see Ephesians chapter two, verses eight and nine, for example – then it wouldn't make a difference who or how one was created to love. It just, it couldn't be a consideration. While one may or may not debate that certain fashion faux pas should or should not[40] be considerations for life everlasting, ultimately, obviously, nothing else matters.

Not eternally.

---

[40] Should.

Like I said, my family has been cool.

Really cool. Cool, in this case, of course, means supportive. Cool, in this case, does not, per se, mean anything such as groovy or neat-o or offspring-approved or to-be-seen-with-in-public or anything such as this[41].

That is, my immediate family has been cool. As far as my extended family is concerned, leaving the Catholic faith was difficult enough. It was honestly the hardest thing I've ever done. And I'll never forget my sweet, devout grandmother quietly leaving the room. She never uttered a word of disapproval, which I appreciated, sure. But with the weight of her departure and the many, many lingering silent moments that followed, well, one knows what kind of damage one has done.

So, it was enough for me, dramatically departing from the denomination of my childhood. As for explaining the rest, as for coming out or anything related?

Maybe later. Maybe someday. There's always tomorrow.

But on the other hand, time is running out. It can all just be so limited; you know?

And I don't do it, I can't do it. I can't bear any more of the silence, but here we are. In hospice, where they send you to await the end.

---

[41] See the third footnote. Definition seven.

I want to say she approved. He approved. Grandma and grandpa died so close together, after all. I want to say they knew the whole time, as do most people, and perhaps they did. But the weight of the departure.

We're all standing around this bed and my grandmother is deeply asleep. And we all know that, to us, anyway, she's already gone. But she's here, physically present and with a chest that moves up and down, and me, I'm with much of my extended family thinking about my grandma and the life she lived, the quiet, honorable life, and I'm thinking about my grandma but, I'm also, for reasons I can't explain, I'm also thinking about Tim. I don't know why, and it seems involuntary, ill-timed and odd but, I just wish he had known her. I wish he had been acquainted with the beautiful woman she was.

And so we all lean down to say our goodbyes. Here, everyone has an opportunity to say whatever they want, a whisper without fear of response, and everyone is leaning in to give a kiss on the cheek or the forehead and it all feels really, really bizarre. Procedural. Our family is huge. Here, in this room, are so many secrets, not merely mine. And here come so many kisses, one by one.

My family, not really the kissing type until now.

I suppose this is an opportunity. I suppose, when it is my turn, I should lean in and my secret should be shared. Some secret. Something to be ashamed of? Something to be proud of? Something some of us are still unsure of.

Anyway of course that's not the secret I share. The line is too long and there are people in front of me and there are people behind me and this whole process is utterly foreign. I say, "I love you grandma." I whisper, "I had a lot of fun." I say other dumb stuff, other meaningless stuff, I probably miss the point entirely, and mostly, I just move out of the way.

Allow the line to progress.

I missed it. I missed her.

I'll miss her.

The tragedy isn't the lack of a tortoise. Okay, it is sad, the lack of a tortoise, because really everyone needs one, but this, this is not tragic. It's just a shame. Such a shame. What else goes in the twenty-gallon tank now that the hamsters[42] have so tragically reached their end?

Fish? Ew.

The tragedy isn't an empty twenty-gallon tank.

The tragedy isn't running out of quarters to play skee-ball, and it isn't the failed pursuit of having enough tickets to trade in for the fifty-piece matchbox car kit complete with race track the size of the above-average living room.

It isn't a want for ice cream after the fried chicken buffet every Sunday only the machine is jammed and probably your mother wants you to go for sugar-free again, anyway. No sprinkles. Also, have you ever noticed the ice-cream machine at McDonald's is always and only broken when you want ice cream from McDonald's? Registered Trademark.

The tragedy, it isn't HAVING TO EAT THE VEGETABLES BEFORE LEAVING THE TABLE.

Okay, it is. But it also isn't.

Just, play along.

---

[42] Tom and Jerry.

No, the tragedy isn't even having to buy a new lunchbox because the one that's lasted six years and was easily the favorite because, duh, it's vintage David Bowie[43], but it doesn't last the move and now it's broken and all this new town has is plain blue or polka dots and who even likes polka dots[44]?

No, none of this is tragic. Not truly. Sad, sure. We all experience sadness but here, now. The tragedy is within the family.

It is exactly what you think it is because the story is the same. It's yours and mine and all of ours, except when it isn't.

It's tragic because it doesn't have to be.

This family is the kind in which Christianity extends to the convicted-but-contrite murderer and it reaches far, so far that its arms are open to the prostitute and the vagabond, the derelict and the destitute, converted, sure, of course, but when the son is gay?

Ah, salvation doesn't reach that far. Not quite.

Except, it does. Doesn't it?

Doesn't it?

---

[43] David Bowie lunchboxes vary widely in price when doing a cursory internet search but mine, mine is going for $38. A real collectible!

[44] This girl, Marcy. She likes polka dots. She wears them every Monday, without fail.

Perhaps it is a matter of perspective, and ultimately, one which the family creates and accepts as its own, but the one living it, the one knowing that nothing can change, that sexuality cannot change, nor should it have to.

This love story, no.

Here, in this story, in their story and in yours, and, in fact, in everyone's, the opportunity for grace and salvation extends. The way it was meant to be.

No, it turns out this story, it has all of the animals and the ice-cream machine works in this story; it works every single time he wants a full-fat, full-sugar, sprinkle-laden gift from above because no, this story, it isn't tragic.

Lack of acceptance is tragic. Lack of acceptance is a choice.

Instead, this story is hilarious and beautiful and brilliant and hopeful, and in it you'll find salvation and honor and peace and happiness and love and joy.

No tragedy here. None.

Not yet.

After hospice, after death, after funeral, my aunt says,

"Did you introduce your friend to grandma?"

[It turns out, I had no idea there was any awareness of a "friend" to introduce anyone to. That is, like Francine, does this aunt know about this (quote-unquote) friend? Does my whole extended family, who knows everything and nothing about me, do they all know about this (italicized) friend? Does everyone on Earth know about this (you-get-the-point) friend[45]?]

So, I just said,

"Uhhhhhhhh.[46]"

On an as-needed basis, I can be exceedingly, exceptionally eloquent. And alliterative.

Then she looked at me and I looked at her and it was that look, a look like we all know and so, I just said,

"Oh. No. I didn't."

She said, without a moment's hesitation, she said,

"Well. I told her."

---

[45] Tim. The friend is Tim. It's Tim.

[46] Full disclosure, it's also entirely possible I said, "Ummmmmm" or similar.

I said,

"Oh."

Additional examples in eloquence and alliteration.

So, she continued,

"I just wanted to talk to her about it. And, do you know what she said?"

Of course, I knew what she said. She said, he's no grandson of mine. She said, that does it, he'll stop receiving timely birthday[47] and Christmas cards from us. She said, his poor, poor parents. My poor, poor daughter. Of course she did.

Only, grandma, according to my aunt, actually, she said,

"I'm happy for him."

My grandmother, she said, "I'm not going to think any differently of him."

She said, "I just want him to be happy."

---

[47] $20 every single year, without fail. Once, my grandma CLEARLY forgot it was my birthday when we visited. She quietly excused herself. Came back with a card, ink still wet. It was adorable. The $20 cashed, just the same.

My aunt, she tells me these things at the funeral, or at, like, the after-funeral thing where everyone is eating. It's some sort of super-weird potluck. This morbid situation where you see all these cousins you never see, and it's just like so-and-so's wedding only somebody really, really important, well, they died and, my aunt, the deceased's daughter, she says,

"I thought you'd want to know."

Sarah is my best friend because she had crackers[48] and I was hungry and, come to find out, I'm a practical person and my friendship is most freely granted when I'm ravenous and you have crackers or, less specifically, food.

Go ahead. Make a note[49].

We went on a field trip freshman year to see a musical in Chicago. We go every year in high school and now, in year three, I am a professional participant and I have a finer understanding of the essential nature of the road-trip nosh. Of course, now I can just rely on Sarah for these things so it might seem the point is moot, but just the same, it's important to me that you know that I've evolved.

Anyway, Sarah was the first person I came out to. And yes, I'm a Christian and regular churchgoer. I suppose, as far as the capital-B Book is concerned, I'm as heaven-bound as they come and I'm really excited about all of that, but one can't live in the closet forever.

After all, closets stifle. There can be moth balls. Holes in sweaters[50]!

---

[48] Triscuits.

[49] Cracked Pepper and Rosemary Triscuits.

[50] Dried lavender is an excellent home remedy. I don't know why I know this. But, you're welcome.

Not to mention, I wear suspenders and purple pants and fuzzy onesies and unicorn buttons. No, not at the same time. Of course not. That would be tacky. Nay, I'm classy, very classy, the classiest, but I'm just illustrating how there's really no closet within which to reside, save for the oblivious, and even then, presumably that is by choice.

Ironic to note that there is a choice in ignoring that which is not a choice.

Irony, but, beyond that, there really is no point.

I'm just here, living my life. The way God intended. The Gospel, with glitter.

A metaphor, of course. Everyone is obviously aware that glitter is the worst. Satan made glitter; one presumes. That's not written anywhere except here and I'm no authority on anything other than household chores such as vacuuming. Vacuuming is the best. Jesus loves vacuuming and that's why glitter is most likely demonic. So that's that. I for one am glad we fleshed that out a bit.

Sarah, also eternity-equipped, didn't appear to know what to say at first. So, she said,

"Eh."

And I thought she couldn't hear me, so I said, a bit louder, I said,

"CAN I HAVE ANOTHER CRACKER?"

And then I asked for her to pass the soda she had, also not mine, because the crackers, they were tasty, but honestly, a bit dry.

But she heard me. The part that immediately preceded the bit about the crackers and the request for a beverage. She heard me and she knew, the whole time, the same as everyone else. She was, after all, anything but daft. She heard me say it, actually say it out loud, and maybe I smiled, even. Maybe I was happy to finally get the word out. Maybe I was happy to share my secret.

Maybe she could tell.

And in her own way, maybe she smiled back.

Maybe.

Pretty quickly after I was visited by my church family and started attending the Baptist church more regularly, I started reading the Bible, faithfully, daily.

Because the Bible is the only book routinely criticized without having been read and because I realize many continue to think of my life as a contradiction, I just kind of needed to know for myself.

And I'll never judge someone for how they think based upon their reading of the Good Book. In fact, all I will say is it IS a good book. In fact, it's a great one. One with plenty of blood and guts and gore, in fact. Action-packed. And sexy[51]. I don't know if that gets me in trouble on college applications or whatever, but it's true.

Go ahead. Read all about it.

And so as much as I love reading, the Bible is the only book I've committed to reading more than once. Otherwise, life's way too short and there's plenty of stuff to read. But this, this one's important. I'll take this one a bit more seriously and I'll read it a bit more often, sure.

(I do not mean to say you can't read the book you currently hold more than once. You can. It won't take you very long. In fact, you can buy multiple copies and read each one of them once, or more than once. Or give them as gifts. They're pretty. Anyway, I'm just saying I would totally allow the exception.)

---

[51] The Bible was on the banned books list put out by the American Library Association in 2015 due to "religious viewpoint." Yes, I think we can laugh at that.

Every day, this Book that I read convinces me to live a beautiful, big, bold life. It tells me to love God and love others. So that's what I will do. I will love God and I will love everyone else that comes my way to the best of my imperfect ability, and, who knows, I may or may not be lucky enough to love one of those people just a bit more deeply. Whoever they are.

Which brings me back to Tim.

Almost.

First, a theatrical interruption.

Up until about two years ago, closet or lack of closet, I was a completely different person. Randomly wandering about. Trying to find someplace to belong. Desperate for someplace to fit in.

And yes, for sure, Jesus has played a giant part in my personal solution.

Also, for sure, leaving middle school helped. Listen, middle school is just a weird time for everyone. It's common knowledge. I mean, I was excellent, truly excellent, for-some-reason-I-may-never-understand excellent, at tetherball[52] in fifth through eighth grade. I don't think people play it much these days, but that's what my middle school had. Basketball hoops and poles with balls attached by ropes. I wasn't going to be able to play basketball as a vertically-challenged individual, so I suppose, naturally, I became a star tetherball athlete. A virtuoso, varsity phenomenon.

I was an athlete. A tetherball star.

Yes, it was a pretty weird time.

In addition to my relationship with Christ, my promotion from middle school, and my athletic prowess, however, upon first arriving at high school, my life was forever, instantly improved by a lady of questionable sanity permanently equipped with a purple pen.

---

[52] A variation of tetherball, played with rackets, is referred to as totem tennis. It is a stupid, stupid game.

You see, I thought the stage was for me but I had no actual talent. And this lady, she was in charge of the theatre department and she was super nice but she also, like, for some reason, appreciated talent.

Weird, I am aware.

So, as the stage became less and less of a possibility for me, at least at first, she found another job for which I qualified. You see, far, far offstage, it would turn out that no one else wanted to compile information, sell advertisements, proofread, and put together the playbill. Add to the fact that we did six shows a year, so, it was a very busy job best suited for talentless folk with the time to devote to writing and producing six ridiculously-detailed pamphlets.

And, okay, I suppose I'm not exactly talentless. As mentioned, I'm super good at tetherball. And, it would turn out, over the course of my high school career, I would be in a few shows, even. Small roles. Walk-ons and bit parts. Even so, I would still, always proofread the program.

Because, for whatever reason, it didn't precisely match my pants, nevertheless, I would learn to love that purple pen. It would turn out, most high schoolers would be scared of it. After all, it's how her papers are graded and her notes are taken and certainly how her edits are made to my program copy, and sure, sometimes the edits are a bit hard to swallow, but even when she yells at you with capital letters, IT'S PURPLE! How fun is that!?

We would spend a lot of time together editing programs.

As a result, she would be the second person I told.

"Mrs. S!"

"Yes." She peeked over these interesting, little half-moon eyeglasses. Spectacles. Like whole glasses were too expensive or something? Anyway, that look, that was when she was deepest in thought and really not to be bothered unless it was the absolute MOST serious of matters.

She lowered the glasses.

I hesitated.

"Do you have any crackers?"

There was no answer to this. I was obviously deflecting. Nerves, I guess. But I was also hungry, and Sarah was nowhere to be found.

Mrs. S kind of sighed, and just as she was about to return her spectacles to her rolling eyes, because, well, time was running out and I was crying wolf...

I spoke again.

"Anyway, I have a thing to say."

"Is this about the program that's due on my desk for final edits in twenty minutes?"

"Yes."

"..."

This is when her eyes and the movement of her glasses did the talking. She was clearly annoyed but always, somehow, sympathetic.

"I think I may have a person. And like, I don't know what I mean, like we just met, but anyway he's pretty great, and I just don't even know what I'm talking about so never mind, ignore all of this, especially the extremely subtle use of gendered pronoun and, well, you may continue raising your spectacles now…"

So that's exactly what she did. Mrs. S slowly raised her spectacles and looked down at the papers in her hand.

And I continued proofing. And she continued grading.

And she said, two minutes and thirty-three excruciating seconds of silence later (I counted), without looking up, without stopping her important and brutal and horrible work, she said:

"Do you know if he's any good at drama?"

And it was true, no kidding, as you already know by now, I had met someone[53].

How it happens is, of course, completely by accident. How it happens is you get tired of keeping secrets, and for a while, sure, you are fine, in fact, more than fine being single, but then, even here, even in high school, when everyone who's anyone is making out in the halls – yes, there are plenty of people that aren't but this is high school and we manufacture some major drama here – and anyway don't you just wonder? Or don't you just want to, don't you just need to know?

Is there someone else like me?

Of course, there is someone else like me.

Absolutely. One hundred percent. There have to be people like me. Thousands of them. Hundreds of them.

Tens of them?

And so you log onto the computer, join the program, create the profile. Because, obviously, the internet has all of the answers. And, of course, it depends on what you believe.

The algorithms just, I don't know, work. They entwine, and they make their matches and you connect on an app and you click or wink or nudge or whatever the case may be and then eventually you realize you should probably talk in real life. Or something.

---

[53] His name is Tim.

It's just, depending on what you believe, maybe the Bible is right. Maybe we aren't really meant to be alone. Whatever that means, sure, it can mean me and Sarah and Mrs. S. We do happen to spend an inordinate amount of time together. And friends are super cool. Teachers can even be super cool. They can also be really, really not cool. I know.

But maybe, for some of us, maybe even a lot of us, we aren't meant to live alone. Iron sharpens iron and all of that.

And yet, Paul was cool with being alone and even encouraged others to join him in that life. But in the same breath, he knew it was a special calling for a select few.

So, the self-proclaimed number one social media site comes out with a friend-finder for teenagers that clearly doubles as platonic-plus – if you know what I mean[54] – and it's this big, splashy promotion and we meet online. I don't necessarily encourage it. High school romance is probably best found in the hallways where everyone is[55] making out[56].

---

[54] You do.

[55] Or is not.

[56] Or is.

And there are all of these ways to search for people and everyone has such an interesting life. At least online. And you can narrow things down based on your own likes and dislikes. For instance, you can say you only want to chat with teens in your area or you can say you're interested in golf and you only want to talk to fellow golfers, only I don't know why you'd want to do that because golf is pretty terrible so that's why I would say anything but golf, please, and I would talk to sensible people.

Okay, so yes. It's weird.

Tim, turns out, was online too.

He was online and he checked the box "Christian" and he also checked the box for "not-a-golfer".

And, I mean, there's also the part about him being stunningly beautiful with the eyes and the teeth and the hair and the face and the decently-keen fashion sense.

And yeah, I think, okay, this could maybe work.

It turns out, beyond the promo, if you pay a special fee or watch an ad or take a quiz or jump through whatever crazy hoops, you can chat with your fellow teenager. Or, you can stalk people in your relatively small town by switching back and forth on this app and other social media and you can find the same picture and you can figure out how to chat without paying a special fee. Not that I'm recommending any of this. Go ahead, pay the fee, watch the ads. I'd hate to upset any potential sponsors.

We seemed to have a lot of the same interests. And he's new to town. And, of all things, he invites me to this tiny, Baptist church.

The conversation online lasts a few days and, even though our school is somewhat large, I do spot him in the hallways. I don't say hi or anything, not immediately. Not yet. He doesn't either. Each night on the internet, however – and not on that app, not any longer, we both agreed that was weird but remained grateful for the initial connection – we were there. Able to chat more freely. Our situations, similar and different.

Anyway, Sunday was soon and, in the words of our fair Fiona, skip ahead, skip ahead. (This is a SHREK: THE MUSICAL reference.)

The bottom line is; it was a match.

A beginning.

The beginning of us.

TIM/ Hi.

CHARLIE/ Hi.

TIM/ We connected on that other app and I felt weird so I switched over to this, is that okay with you?

CHARLIE/ Oh yeah. That app is weird. I was just, I don't know. Trying it out. Every day. For three or four or five or six or seven months.

TIM/ Hahah, I just moved here. I think I've seen you around but IDK. I saw you were a Christian too. I'm interested in hearing more about that. My dad's a pastor.

CHARLIE/ Oh wow, did you move here for a church?

TIM/ Kind of, yeah. It's Calvary Baptist, the small church on Sangamon. You know it?

CHARLIE/ Definitely. I go to youth group there. I haven't been to a service because I still go to Catholic church on the weekends. We squeeze it into our Netflix queue.

TIM/ I'll see you at youth group! And school. I'd love to hang out. And, if you want, you can come to church with me. Haha, I think my parents would like to see me evangelizing. *eye roll emoji*

CHARLIE/ OMG I totally got evangelized to AFTER my first youth group meeting there! My mom sorta says I was brainwashed. She'd freak out if I switched churches. But, honestly, I think I like the stuff I'm getting at youth group more than at church. So I'm in! Let me know when I can rebel. I suppose we should meet first.

TIM/ Yeah. Let's!

CHARLIE/ You could always come to drama club after school. I sort of live there...

Meanwhile, adolescing in the theatre has its perks.

And I won't lie. It's true. It's obvious and it's true. The only reason he shows up is because I make him. I don't even know why he listens to me[57].

"YES, it's cool, I say. No, for real. It's great fun. And you don't have to do anything if you don't want to. Look, Mrs. S, she switches it up all the time. Sometimes it's improvisations where you just pretend like you're some kind of plant or animal, or, if you aren't feeling it, you just say I'm a dead worm and you just lie on the ground, or you can even be an alive worm because they don't really move anyway unless it's newly rained so you can be an alive worm during a drought and you can just, like, I dunno, every once in a while, lift your head or slide or something. HONESTLY JUST TAKE A NAP ON THE FLOOR IT'S SO FINE."

Naps are a very, very good negotiating tactic, I find. Nobody doesn't like napping. Generally speaking, faking a nap is like a totally legal way of not paying attention to anyone or anything and absolutely, but politely, not caring about your surroundings. I think even doctors are recommending it.

Here's to our health.

As if he wasn't already convinced, I went on with the benefits of our after-school theatrical pursuits. There are many. Following is only the most important.

---

[57] Of course I do. I can be VERY persuasive.

"Mrs. S actually feeds us. And, none of these healthy, after-school snacks like, I don't know, yogurt or corn chips and not those generic, nearly-creamless-left-of-Oreo atrocities[58]. These are your on-brand, special-occasion snacks. This is crackers and cheese so fine you might as well serve them with the frilly toothpicks. Thank you, we will. Charcuterie. That's right."

The theatre, around here, it's for improvisations and *proper* snacking.

Snacks and napping and here he is.

Mrs. S has us workshopping the spring musicale. It's okay. I mean, the show will be double or triple cast and every single human being who can walk and chew gum at the same time, or who can just walk or who can just chew gum or who even at least attempts to do either will be cast. Inclusive to the extreme. And that's cool. Really cool.

The gum, after all, it deserves to be chewed. Unless it's that gross gum at the checkout counter that portends to tastes like dessert. Nope. IT. IS IN NO WAY. TIRAMISU. And it is three calories for a reason. Just, nope. Stop it right now. This instant.

But this musicale, this show that she's chosen, it's only that it's a love story. And there are two male leads.

---

[58] It seems to me that generic Oreos are less than two dollars cheaper than regular Oreos. Instead of saving money this way, I don't know about you, but I urge MY mother to go for quantity discounts. I think you can buy, as an example, fourteen bags of regular Oreos and they will average out to each be less than two dollars cheaper than buying one bag of regular Oreos. It's the same math, really.

No no, it's not like that. This novel is easy, but it's not that easy.

Two male leads, two female leads. Your average (if we were being honest, sub-average) rom-com, if you will, only the song-and-dance kind. An old chestnut, as it were. I'm only saying, it's not necessarily my kind of show.

And yet, here we are. Me, I'm here for the cheese[59]. Sarah, she's here to be the lead. And she will be. Duh. But what would it be if I could convince Mrs. S that he and I? Well, he and I, you see, we're very much the leading men type. The stuff main characters of coming-of-age novels are made of. Bildungsroman. That is a great word.

Anyway, it all comes down to the audition. And that's in two weeks. As a reminder, I'm more or less a talentless hack with a flair for editing programs.

Feel free to skip ahead to where he gets a lead and I watch elatedly from the curtain.

---

[59] Preferably Colby Jack or Pepperjack, other jacks are just fine. Turns out, I'll eat just about anything that isn't blue. Blue cheese tastes like hairspray and not the fun, dreamy Link Larkin, musicale kind.

TIM/ You weren't kidding. Snacks were on point. Mom was a little weirded out when I didn't want any dinner.

CHARLIE/ You didn't eat dinner? I don't, I'm sorry, that's just not a feeling with which I can identify.

TIM/ I ate an inhuman amount of cheese.

CHARLIE/ That's what pooping is for.

TIM/ I think, I'm maybe going to choose not to respond to that, if that's okay. However, if I were to respond I would say something like I think cheese might hinder that ability, actually[60]. But I'm not. I'm actively refusing. I'd delete all of this, in fact, but that seems difficult. Akin to post-cheese pooping. IRONY! You going to youth group tomorrow?

CHARLIE/ Honestly, thank you for the education[61]. And, for sure, for sure. Of course I'm going! You'll eat there, won't you? I mean. You do eat?

TIM/ Yes. Cheese today. Pizza tomorrow. It's a wonder I still fit into these clothes[62].

CHARLIE/ Tell me about it. Pants are tight enough as it is these days. That's the fashion though. So they tell me.

---

[60] It seems that an overconsumption of cheese can cause diarrhea, actually. And, maybe, acne. Not fun, sure, but these are risks that, at time of writing, I'm willing to consider.

[61] Miseducation! Fake News!

[62] An overconsumption of dairy products CAN lead to bloating. So, this part of the transcript seems to hold up fairly well, actually.

TIM/ Yeah, all eight of my pockets are full right now. You'd be so embarrassed.

CHARLIE/ I hate that so I'm going to ignore it, but like ACTUALLY ignore it (unlike you, as noted above) but also secretly judge, just a little. So, you're going to audition?

TIM/ Are you?

CHARLIE/ I mean, yes, I'll audition. Mrs. S. basically makes me. I don't know why. I'll be fine in the chorus. You, however. You're made to be a lead.

TIM/ Ha! Well, I'll keep the script in one of my many, many pockets. I'll let you know.

CHARLIE/ Hate…

TIM/ Love.

CHARLIE/ Byeeeeeeeee.

Honestly, no kidding, I just read about a man who picked up sticks on a Sunday and was subsequently stoned to death[63].

So, apparently that's a thing.

Can you imagine? I mean, I CLEARLY don't pick up sticks very often, but when I do, I don't stop to think about the day of the week before so doing.

And, yes, I realize this is a historical and/or cultural thing. First of all, we don't stone people to death anymore. Here, anyway[64]. That would seem a step backward, humanely speaking, and also, these days, we paint rocks and lose them to be rediscovered as an act of kindness.

Yesterday's weapons. Today's treasures.

Reading the Bible daily is just a good habit for me, an excellent way to start the day.

Believe it or not, whatever you think about it, I submit that it's worth reading. After all, book by book, it has to be worth some serious AR points[65].

---

[63] Numbers 15:32-26

[64] Not to bring down the mood but, in some countries, apparently one can be stoned to death for being homosexual!

[65] On its official website, the Bible isn't listed on its own, but instead, a cursory search provides AR points for each book. For example, the book of Numbers, in the New International Version, is worth five AR points. Judges, in the same version, is worth three points. Someone could calculate the entire book this way, or someone could just, you know, read it.

And, if you're paying attention, every once in a while, a man gets stoned to death for picking up sticks on the Sabbath.

Sticks and stones...

I think the point is, times have changed. Cultures have changed. People have changed. Pretty much everything has changed since the time of writing of the scriptures. And now we don't stone people[66]. And for some reason, these days, people consume shellfish. By choice. Seriously, I have watched my dad eat oysters. Slurp, more like.

Evolution? Progress? I honestly wonder.

And we don't hire slaves and we don't silence women.

And, maybe, just maybe, men can love men. Women can love women.

---

[66] Again: here.

Or, maybe, just maybe, actually and for real, men always have been able to love men and women always have been able to love women, and, oh, also by the way, men always have been able to love women and women always have been able to love men, and, maybe, just maybe, that's the way it was since the beginning of time (only now we're less related to each other) and maybe, just maybe, that continues to be okay today and on and on into forever, for all of history and for all of the future and maybe, just maybe, the only thing that's actually changed over time and over pages and over all of history has been perception or tolerance or acceptance or whatever we're calling it today[67].

Wouldn't that be something?

Translation aside, I suppose the only thing that hasn't changed are the words themselves. And maybe context becomes worthy of our consideration.

Read all about it.

---

[67] The word maybe is used seventy times in this book, more than ten times in this sentence alone. Sorries!

I don't want to mislead. I truly am a simple person. But it's not always the crackers[68] that get me.

Today, Mrs. S promises chocolate chip cookies and she delivers, as I knew she would, with the nearest bakery's finest confections. They're a dream. They're one of those not too crunchy, not burnt, but not too soft, and also no nuts because this is not intended to be some kind of tragic cry-fest, and, we want readers with allergies involved, and well, basically, we can simply say that these are the kinds of cookies Jesus provides in the afterlife[69]. I assume. The Book doesn't say, insofar as I am aware.

Anyway, he doesn't even like chocolate chip cookies, he says. And I tell him, this is why this arrangement works because I'll eat yours. I'll make the necessary sacrifices. This is something that I can do.

Here we are at the pre-audition workshop. Here, laid out in front of us all, are sides of music and pieces of dialogue from the show. He looks horrified. It's understandable. I'm making him do all of this, only, I'm not actually making him do any of this. Of course I'm not. He wants to be here. Cookie or no cookie. He looks, I dunno, happy. Subsequently, I'm happy. For me, it's the cookie but it's also, undeniably him.

---

[68] Triscuits are still the preferred cracker, but my mind is open should availability be limited.

[69] I like a cookie that is slightly undercooked, actually. Moist, maybe, though I understand that word to be triggering to many.

"EVERYBODY ONSTAGE NOW[70]!"

And then there's this massive rush of people finishing cookies and making lines onstage, and it's our own version of a cattle call only a terribly organized one, like one in which the bovines probably stampede all over each other and not in some cool, Riverdance-meets-Rockette sort of way, and, anyway, Mrs. S just keeps shouting and no one knows what to do and we're all running around and I'm holding someone's hand.

I'm holding his hand. BUT ONLY BECAUSE HE NEEDS TO KNOW WHERE TO GO.

Um. Obviously.

He stops and he looks at me and he shakes his head and he forces his hand out of mine and he runs off. Offstage left, for the record.

And he's just, gone, like some kind of horrible magic trick. Only one in which the magician has moved the curtain or opened the door or lifted the lid two or three times looking for the assistant to reappear after a fabulous surprise costume change only they don't. He doesn't.

He never comes back.

---

[70] Mrs. S notably doesn't need a bullhorn for this. Our auditorium is large, sure, but, also, everyone is nervousably silent. It's a power move, clearly. I guess we can all appreciate that. Also, I might have made up the word nervousably just now. I think I like it!

He doesn't consider himself an actor.

He does consider himself a Christian.

He, on the other hand, considers himself both for, after all, one is an actor as soon as one is willing to stand onstage even if it is just to clear his throat and begin to say a line and start crying. Only a little.

Anyway, his mother loved his performance.

Christians.

Christians and men.

Boys.

Men.

In the theatre and in high school and into each other.

Certainly, defying stereotypes, but what are the stereotypes even for if not to be defied?

Like gravity[71].

Cue the music.

One supposes, this whole thing, all of their lives, everything they've been and everything they will be, thus far, they've been in defiance of something.

Just not Jesus.

---

[71] This is a WICKED reference. WICKED is a musical and if you don't know that – don't worry, this book can still be for you – but you should stop reading this. Put the bookmark in it. Dog-ear it if you have to but don't do that if you borrowed it from your local school or public library which just saved you twelve dollars and ninety-seven cents. Or so. Anyway, head to your favorite cellular smartphone music listening application and do some searching. Then come back. You're welcome.

He doesn't even look at me at youth group. And, I have to tell you just in case it's not obvious, it hurts and its upsetting and these are kind of new feelings for me and, anyway, I deflect.

"Sarah, why are we even here[72]?" I ask.

"Well, sir, you see, I don't know why you're here. Just kidding, I know why you're here. Tim's over there. Anyway, I'm here because there's pizza[73] and games and, honestly, rebellion," she suggests.

"Rebellion? This is church," I say.

Sarah responds, "Yeah, my family. Your family. Catholic. This, notsomuch."

"Oh, right right right. Okay, that makes total sense. I do like a little rebellion, once in a while. But why isn't he even looking at us or talking to us or acknowledging us or, I don't know..." I wonder.

"Making out with us?" Sarah interjects.

"Ew. No. No. No. No. Ew. No."

"Okay, apparently that was a bit much for you?" she says.

---

[72] I mean, *besides* pizza, obviously.

[73] See?

"I mean, yes. But also. No. For the record, you said making out with US. *That* is ew. I mean, me, on the other hand[74]. I mean, still no. Not right now. No. Nope. But probably less ew."

And Sarah says, "Whatever, look, I'm just saying that I'm here for some dollar pizza and you, you are too but also, for now, probably you should go talk to Tim."

He really is talking to no one. Standing by no one. Looking at no one. So, I go over. Slowly, because if this doesn't look like it's going to work out, I can easily divert to the bejeweled bathroom. No one would know the difference. Except it would probably be super obvious and incredibly embarrassing, but it's still definitely something I can do.

I can walk and chew gum at the same time.

He does look over. He looks over. He's looking over and the eyes that I'm getting, they're not angry eyes. These aren't fighting eyes only, what are they? Wounded? Am I looking at shame and embarrassment? What am I seeing?

He walks away but not quickly, as if to be followed, so I do that, I look back at Sarah and shrug my shoulders and I head towards the hallway with him and as soon as we're there he says sorry. He says he's not sure drama club is for him.

Well. Drama club is for everyone who likes classy snacking and naptime, I counter. But my tired, old standbys might not be working anymore.

---

[74] Ew?

I plead, "Listen, I won't grab your hand anymore. Honestly, I was just trying to lead you in the right direction. I didn't even notice I was doing it and I really..."

"I liked it[75]," Tim says.

"...I really, really didn't mean to and I mean it's definitely something I would probably, likely do for anyone and, wait. What's that?"

And Tim says, "I liked you holding my hand, okay. And I wanted to continue doing that and then I noticed people were looking and people are from church and people are from school and my classes and people will talk and this is a really small town and my dad is the pastor of this church and I just. I can't. I don't know. I don't think..."

"Okay. But in just rewinding a little, tiny bit, you did, just, for the record, say you liked it[76]?" I ask.

"Yes. I liked holding your hand. I want to hold your hand. But not like a Beetle's song. Only, I guess, maybe kind of like the Beetle's song. I don't know. That's cheesy and the song is old so."

"Yeah, so, not typically my genre, but I can totally vibe. If that's something people still say," I say.

---

[75] Oh?

[76] So, definitely, absolutely, *not* ew!

Tim replies, "It isn't[77]. Look, I don't know what I'm saying. I don't know what we're doing. I have no idea what this brief musical analysis has been. I just. I can't do it here. Listen, can you just leave me alone for a while?"

"Oh. Yeah, sure. Are you still going to audition?" I ask hopefully.

Tim says, "I'll be there. Yeah, I guess, if my parents let me. I suppose I'll see you there."

"Cool. So, do you want to go bowling?" Satisfied for now, I change the subject.

"Yeah. But I don't want to ride the bus," says Tim.

"Oh yeah. For sure, me neither. Super not cool," I say. "I'll drive."

---

[77] People still TOTALLY say vibe. Don't they?

Let's go!

Ok, but it looks like we need to stop at the gas station first. It'll just take a second, he says, but he really thinks he needs some windshield washer fluid because it's going to rain. I argue this doesn't make a lot of sense and worry we are wasting three dollars and twenty-four cents, after tax, that could be spent on shoe rentals and French fries. After all, if it is raining, if liquid is falling from the sky, will it not very likely fall upon your windshield and, assuming as much, would it not be quite unnecessary and even, perhaps, an impediment, of sorts, to place more liquid upon said surface? But he said I was an idiot and, essentially, no one talks like this and he spent the three dollars and twenty-four cents.

After tax.

I just hope we can still afford French fries. Not to mention, dipping sauce costs extra[78]. Cruel, cruel world.

Bowling makes me hungry, which I think is logical because it is a sport and involves physical activity, which means I will be burning calories which means I will need to consume calories and, just me, but I might as well do my best to make sure these calories are super delicious.

---

[78] This is actually, as a matter of fact, ridiculous. One should get as much sauce as one needs and it should be included in the price of the product requiring said accoutrement. No one is arguing consumption of naked French fries as appropriate, after all. A condiment-less fry is not an option. Duh.

He says bowling is probably considered a sport, sure, but he questions the actual amount of physical exertion and is so brazen as to contest that, indeed, were I to be engaging in meaningful exercise, it would certainly behoove me to ingest in healthy calories as I expend them. He suggests the vegetable medley.

I said, behoove is a cool word. It should be used more often. I also said no bowling alley actually serves vegetable medleys. To even suggest such a thing is surely some kind of sacrilege.

Not long after we exit the gas station, we pass the youth group bus, which we think is hilarious.

Suckers.

It doesn't take long, indeed, for the rain to start pouring down.

The bowling alley is about an eight-mile drive that maybe takes twelve minutes to complete, eleven depending on lights.

Six and a half, if you drive like him.
Speeding down a highway[79], speeding past the more prudent drivers of church busses, turns out, is all fun and games until you hit a rather massive puddle of water.

What happens next happens very quickly.

---

[79] 74 miles per hour in a 65 mile per hour zone. To be precise.

First, the car spins in a circle, maybe two circles, or ovals, something that feels vaguely round, I don't know, I'm not a geometrical genius. Whatever the shape and however many of them, this is when you begin shouting most of the words you're not necessarily supposed to say per Tim's dad's sermon and mom's pre- and post-sermon analyses.

Second, once geometric shapes have been exhausted, the car leaves the ground, exits the highway, departs from the planet. Defies gravity[80].

Briefly.

Third, the car joins the circus and does a number of flips. Turnovers, neat little tricks.

I think this is when I blacked out.

I do remember the impact. I remember hitting the ground, the middle of the highway. The grassy part in between the two roads, the four lanes.

I remember awakening.

I remember being upside down and unable to move. This was curious.

It didn't take me long to realize that Tim was nowhere to be found.

And this was when I freaked out, not when I noticed I couldn't move, not when I felt the impact of the crash.

---

[80] See previous note regarding the musical, WICKED.

When I lost my, my. Friend. Quote unquote.

This was when I started screaming for help.

Unbuckling my seatbelt made me fall out of my seat and I realized the car was upside down and I was on the roof. Inside. I was now free to move about, with the exception of my head. It took a moment to realize that my head was caught between the top of the seat and the roof of the car.

That was inconvenient.

Shouting and knocking began at my door. Or, it could have been happening the whole time, but this was when I noticed.

Tim, it turned out, essentially swam out of the windshield. He didn't swim. That's not correct. He crawled through a puddle. We would come to refer to it as swimming because that's more dramatic and we're students of the theatre, after all.

This exit was made possible because the windshield was shattered. Clean, though, at a cost of French fries[81] and bowling shoes.

A waste of three dollars and twenty-four cents. I was correct.

For the record.

And somehow, we were both completely fine.

---

[81] I like ranch, but I can settle for honey mustard or, in an absolute worst-case scenario, if there's absolutely nothing else, regular mustard. In no way will I ever dip a fry in catsup. Speaking of ew. Just. Ew.

I was just caught on the roof of the car when I noticed the water was rising.

Turns out, it was pouring. The car was slowly, very slowly and only slightly, sinking into the ground.

The bus passed us, not knowing who was crashed upside down in the middle of the interstate.

The pastor's son, two of their church friends.

They went bowling.

We would have been there, but we were having car troubles.

Tim ran, so I'm told, actually ran INTO ONCOMING TRAFFIC, to flag someone down for assistance because he couldn't get my door open.

The fireman who eventually came, the only thing he said to me was, "this is going to be loud as hell, son." And then he turned on the jaws of life. Which are neat little things that cut up cars, apparently.

The fireman, to his credit, was accurate in his assessment of noise levels.

These were loud scissors.

We were transported to the hospital via an ambulance even though, miraculously, thank the Lord, we were both fine.

That is to say, we could have driven ourselves.

I was hungry. The hospital had French fries and they couldn't have been that subpar to bowling alley food, let's be honest with ourselves.

Our parents picked us up at the hospital. Until then, for a few hours, we had the room to ourselves.

Separate beds, of course.

"Do you know what else I love?" I ask.

Here we are, in our respective hospital beds, eating our respective French fries, having our respective vitals checked what seems like every seventeen minutes even though they're always and always perfectly normal, two crash victims, not a care in the world aside from inadequate dipping-sauce quantities *and* qualities.

"You mean, besides so-called high fashion and, uh, shemomedjamo-ing?" He says, lying right next to me, I should remind you.

"Hmmm, an interesting gerund. Still, more than a bit of a reach on that one. I think, if you didn't drop the o, it would be hyphenated. That's what I was going to say: I love hyphens. Do you know, there's a restaurant in town that has an egg-in-a-hole on its menu? THREE hyphens. Now that, that is special." I've never really told this to anyone because, yes, I'm aware of the level of nerdom we've reached, even for a linguaphile.

"Is it just a piece of toast and an egg though[82]?" Tim offers, practically.

"Well. When you say it like that[83]," I say, somewhat dejected.

"I mean I'm just mentioning what the special menu item actually consists of and how they might, in fact, be two of the commonest things that exist within the realm of breakfast," he continues.

---

[82] It is.

[83] It is.

"Okay that just hurts."

I leave a bit of silence after this statement. Not too much, but just enough to where my bunkmate might believe in my make-believe wounds. But for an instant.

"However, also." I continue because I have to. "My absolute favorite thing about hyphens is typing them. Have you ever noticed that they're small until you press the spacebar? Like, I don't know, baby hyphens. And then they grow up! They mature. Lengthen. You know?"

Tim is silent again. I believe this to be of the contemplative sort. We should sit in it awhile. It feels nice.

Our vitals are checked.

"That might be among the dumbest things I've ever heard in my entire life."

His parents arrive first.

They say hello. Politely. I think because they have to. I'm in the first bed, after all. Mrs. Timoth smiles at me, but that's about it. They make sure that Tim is okay, and he mentions that I am also okay.

It feels a little weird, I guess. Upon first meeting, I felt like his parents liked me. We just came from church, which should honestly delight them both. And, not that it matters, but I wasn't driving. They can't blame me for this accident, can they? I mean I'm sure I can be plenty distracting. Maybe I talked him out of riding the bus, but can they even know that? I think he was just trying to make me feel better, like it was part of his apology or something.

What did he say to them on the phone? I try to think back to our phone calls. Mine involved way too much shrieking from mom. His seemed brief as well. Nothing major.

Whatever the case, there is no more conversation and there certainly is no offer to take me home. No real goodbye.

Tim looks back at me as he leaves. He says, "yeah, okay, fine, baby hyphens are cool."

I smile.

I am victorious.

I am alone.

My vitals are checked[84].

---

[84] Shockingly, they're normal.

He doesn't show up to the audition.

Of course, he doesn't. At least, not right away.

As for me, my audition is horrible. Of course it is. This is why I provide invaluable program edits. I'm not even mad about the audition either. I'll be in the chorus or I'll be triple cast as some kind of one-line character and that will be super great. Mother will love it, and she will cry, and she will bring me flowers, and she will cry, and she will hug me afterwards like seventeen relatives suddenly died and she is so pleased that I was not among them, and she will cry.

Sarah, unsurprisingly, was breathtaking. She will easily land one of the major parts. And I just know that when Tim shows up, if he shows up, he will also nail it. And watching them both fill the stage in their leading roles will be absolutely amazing.

So, Sarah and I sit in the center of the second row while many, many others show up to audition one right after another and I start to realize that maybe I'm not the worst of the lot.

"Is Tim coming?" She says, finally.

"Well, last I knew he was," I respond. "It's an open call. He knows that. He'll show up, I mean, assuming his parents give him their blessing."

"Literally," Sarah says.

"What? Oh, like a pastor thing. So, it's literal because his dad blesses people. I totally get it. Good joke," I say sarcastically[85].

"Right, it was funny. Why aren't you laughing? You always laugh at me. I'm hilarious," Sarah correctly states.

"You are. Talented, hilarious, beautiful. Bride material, truly." I say, "Remember when you made me promise to marry you? Like Artie[86] and Tina in Glee? Yeah, you know that's not actually a thing, right? Anyway, I don't know. I guess I'm just bummed about Tim not being here. Drama is less fun today. I mean, even the cookies are stale."

"The cookies are usually stale," she says, once again, correctly[87]. "He'll show."

Sarah grabs my hand. It's a comforting gesture. Feels much different than holding hands with Tim in this same space just a few days ago. Still, the effect is, overall, positive.

And of course, she's correct. Talented, hilarious, beautiful, and correct. Tim walks in during the third and final hour of auditions, a little bit like he owns the place. Mrs. S looks relieved. And she should be. After seeing the male turnout, I would be too.

---

[85] I'm still not entirely sure this is a good joke. Can you use literally here? Is it funny if you do?

[86] Gay. Kevin McHale is gay. Artie is gay.

[87] That one time, though. The cookies were moist. Delicious. I promise.

But he only says, "Mrs. S, I just wanted to thank you for allowing me to participate in drama club this year. I just wanted you to know that I can't try out. I'm so sorry."

And, again, he's just gone. He doesn't even give her a chance to respond. I don't even know why he bothered showing up at all. He didn't even look at us.

He didn't even look at me.

On Sunday, at church, Tim continues to ignore my presence. It's beginning to hurt. Okay, so it has hurt the entire time. At this point, it's just about to reach the level of absurdity and maybe I'm even getting a little mad about it.

"Hey, can I talk to you for a second?"

"I don't really have time. Mom has me leading Sunday School in ten," he states matter-of-factly.

"Cool." But, it isn't. I respond, "Is that years, days, hours, minutes, or seconds? Either way, I'll take less than ten. Five, even. Two?"

"Minutes. Okay, sure, of course." He gives in. "What's up?"

"Uh, so, I guess that's MY question? I feel like, you know, after we almost died together, I haven't really seen you. So…yeah, what's up?"

"Oh. Well, lots of stuff. I mean, I'm doing great things at school. Oh, I'm in Key Club now. THERAPY. Therapy is[88]…"

I interject, "why were you online?"

"Wait, what?" He says, caught off-guard.

---

[88] Illegal.

"Why did you make a profile online? I mean, we found each other, right? Online. I was online so I could find someone. Someone like me. Someone to, you know, enjoy being around. Maybe more. I know it's just high school, but, honestly, why do it if you're just going to ignore it?" I ask.

To which, he replies, "I'm not ignoring anything."

"You aren't? So, this morning in this church that I'm, that I keep visiting WHO KNOWS WHY – just guessing but probably not Francine's hospitality[89] over there – you totally, definitely acknowledged that I was present, and, that's right, you for sure waved hello and in drama the other day, well, you did seem to very suddenly drop out, and it obviously wasn't because of me, and, oh yeah, you actually totally said hey to Sarah and I. That was really nice of you. Thanks for not, I don't know, DRAMATICALLY walking in and out in two seconds and failing to know I exist ever since."

"What can I say, the snacks weren't up to par in drama club after all, I guess," he says.

"Well, that's true. That was a bit of a bait and switch on my part, I suppose." But I need to know, so I say again, "What's going on, actually?"

"Okay, so, I don't know. I'm just, listen, mom and dad are on my back and I deleted my entire online presence, so thanks for bringing that up. And now there's no social media at all, not even anything normal and…"

---

[89] Ok but if she makes the fried chicken, I should actually admit that it's delicious. Well done, judgmental chicken lady. Well. Done.

"Normal. So, what, how we met. Who we are? That wasn't *normal*?"

"I don't think that's what I meant," Tim says.

"I think it was. Meeting me wasn't normal. I'm not normal. Got it."

"What? No, I."

But I left. It was my turn for a dramatic exit, and honestly, I have no idea what he said after that.

CHARLIE/ Saudade.

CHARLIE/ It's another cool word.

CHARLIE/ Not that you care. Not that you'll ever see this. I don't, I don't really know how that works. If you're not online, that is. Probably there will never be a record of this and, anyway, I'm not sure I want there to be.

CHARLIE/ Anyway, it means wanting something that doesn't exist.

CHARLIE/ You know, like this relationship. This non, this non-relationship.

CHARLIE/ Probably won't ever, actually exist.

CHARLIE/ Kummerspeck. Emotional overeating. I think it has something to do with bacon, but one begets the other. So, that's what these pretzels are for. Not that I don't love bacon. Nobody doesn't love bacon. It's like one of three universal truths. Jesus. Bacon. Fashion. Probably in that order. Anyway, it's only that I'm super hungry, and, anyway, pretzels are healthier than bacon and I'm really trying to work on my figure. You see.

CHARLIE/ For the next guy.

CHARLIE/ That's not true. Okay so now I really hope you never see this. This is bad. Anyway thanks for taking a passing interest in my vocabulary. It's been really great chatting with you, but now I'm thirsty so I need to go get some water or something.

CHARLIE/ Pretzels. They make you thirsty[90]. Probably another universal truth. No one ever ate a bag of pretzels and said, chewing and chewing, you know what I don't need? Glorious, tasteless, life-saving liquid.

CHARLIE/ Talking to yourself is kind of therapeutic. I guess this is like journaling for the tech-savvy? I'm not, definitely not savvy. But it's a cool word. Self: add it to the list.

CHARLIE/ Savvy[91].

CHARLIE/ Kummerspeck[92].

CHARLIE/ Saudade[93].

---

[90] There's a Seinfeld episode about this. I think it's Kramer. He says, "these pretzels are making me thirsty." I'm not sure what else happens in that episode. Probably nothing. The situation is probably never resolved. The whole show is about nothing. So probably nothing actually happens. In any case, Kramer is correct. Pretzels. They make you thirsty. Factual.

[91] Shrewdness and practical knowledge.

[92] Literally means, "grief bacon"

[93] A feeling of longing, melancholy, or nostalgia…

He was a man of God.

And he was a man of God.

One of them, confident in his Christianity. Maybe someone who didn't understand why they were the way they were, but, nevertheless, one that felt reasonably confident that he was who he was or, if not confident, at least something resembling happy.

The other, ever-less confident. The other, feeling more and more pressure to fake it, more and more pressure to exist somewhere else, in some kind of heterosexual haze for the rest of forever or, failing that, to lock away an opportunity to love someone else someplace far, far away and throw away the key.

One of them, feeling ready and able to love the other, or at least, like, in whatever kind of high school capacity romance was available.

The other, maybe, maybe not, ready to do away with it all in favor of some kind of therapy.

Who knows, maybe this time it would work[94].

---

[94] SPOILER ALERT: It won't.

"Congrats on the play[95]," Tim says, passing Sarah in the hall.

"Thanks! I mean, it's not exactly the leading lady, per se. But it'll do in a pinch. Did you see Chuck's part?" She asks.

"Chuck? Is that, are we calling him Chuck now?"

"I thought I'd try it out. Do you think he'll hate it? I don't know. He's in a mood. I'm trying to think of something to help him out. Maybe he wants to try a new personality. For his new profile."

"Wait, Chuck's…Charles is online again?" Tim asks Sarah.

"Oh yeah. Sorry, you didn't know?"

"No…I mean, of course…good for him. Anyway, I just, I wanted to say congrats. I miss you guys," Tim says.

"I…we miss you too."

"Yeah, it sounds like it."

To say this is getting awkward would not be wrong. To say they both had someplace to be before the pending bell would also not be incorrect. Tim nods and attempts a hasty exit when Sarah reaches for his arm.

---

[95] It's a musicale, also known as a musical, of course, but we forgive Tim this misnomenclature.

"Hey, he's just hurting right now. I mean, if you're interested in talking to him, I can try to catch him for you. He started working out. I'm pretty sure it's really weird. So yeah. Obviously, something is wrong. Actually, it's probably mostly your fault."

"Thanks for that," he says.

"Listen, you guys are in a really weird place. Why don't I talk to him and see if I can get him to talk to you or something? Would that, I mean would you be up for that?"

Charles at a gym? Sarah at a gym?!

"Oh, hi.

Tell him I'm fine[96].

Tell him I'm at the gym and I'm fine[97].

Make sure he knows that I'm at the gym because that might score me some points with all of my followers and, anyway, make sure he knows I've absolutely, in no way, gone crazy and, in fact, ever-informed by targeted social media advertisements, I am at the gym because it is free for teens to work out for a limited time, so tell him all of that proves I'm very *normal* in spite of the fact that you and I both know that social media obviously, clearly, and in a very real way, has no idea who they're targeting.

So.

I'm fine[98].

I'm at the gym and I'm fine[99].

Well, you can go.

Well, wait.

---

[96] He isn't.

[97] He *really* isn't.

[98] Nope.

[99] For sure, definitely not.

Okay, no, don't wait. Still go, but tell him even though I'm fine[100] when I'm done with the gym I'm just going to go home and stare at the computer or something so if he, in fact, is not fine I should be home in twelve minutes and forty-three seconds. Add the two-minute cool down. Yes, fourteen forty-three. And counting! I think. Anyway.

Ok, now, I mean, I guess you can go. Unless you like these running machines and brought a change of clothes. Then you could always stay."

I don't see a change of clothes, and I know, if I know anything, *I know* Sarah is not for the treadmill any more than I am, as a general rule, but, she stays.

They who run alongside you, free trial aside, they are the anatomy of a true friend.

Indeed.

"It's just, I can't go back in the closet," I explain, through heavy breathing. I'm running way too fast.

"Why don't we, first of all, why don't we walk? Let's just walk. Because at the speed at which you're running, you're going to fly off of this thing, and, also, through heavy breathing, you're actually shouting, and, like, I'm just not sure you want this private conversation broadcast throughout this entire gymnasium place thing," Sarah says.

---

[100] ...

I take a look around, and no one is directly looking at me, but those without headphones in, okay, they definitely may have heard a lot of this.

I set my speed to turtle[101].

"Thank you. You're always looking out for me."

"I am," she says.

"Also, very direct."

"Yes."

"Okay, so, anyway, Tim clearly doesn't want to act like he knows me in public which, at first, I could do, or at least, I tried to go along with, but I can't do it anymore. At the end of the day, it's his to decide," I say, "but he needs to decide."

"Let me just try to talk to him."

"I think that's good. But, just. If you could..." I begin.

"Anything."

---

[101] The machines do not have an actual turtle setting so, this is based on the presumption that turtles are slow. One could further presume, then, that the fastest setting is rabbit, and then one could infer a sort of tortoise and hare thing. Or, perhaps, the fastest setting is a cheetah? Cheetahs are known to be the fastest land animal, after all. Charlie is no cheetah, though the alliteration is sublime.

"Don't forget to mention the fact that I was working out and probably, just as a casual aside, you could mention the approximate speed at which I was running. I think it was, like, a four and a half[102] or something. Anyway, I could run faster. I couldn't. But, maybe tell him that I could anyway."

"Uh huh. I'll tell him," she says.

"Eight minutes and thirteen seconds."

"I'm on it. Just, um, how do I get off this thing?"

---

[102] See. Numbers, not animals. Treadmill companies should look into the animal thing, however. I might be more inclined to run. Probably not, but it sounds fun...

They were falling apart.

They weren't.

That's too dramatic.

But they kind of were. In a situational comedy sort of way.

He was about to confess. Father's orders.

He was going to keep working out and keep going online and keep assembling pamphlets and hanging around backstage and singing with the chorus and just doing everything he could to not get stuck. He's been stuck before.

They weren't falling apart. That's too dramatic. Even for a theatrical piece.

It's just, they were in different places. And maybe it was too much, too soon.

He thinks it's over.

He's sure it isn't. Unless it is.

"Hey," Tim says.

"Hey," I say.

"I'm sorry," he says.

"It's cool," I say.

No conversation ever goes like this. This one didn't either. Not really. These were the words that were spoken, but none of it believable. All of it, contrived.

Nobody was actually saying anything.

"Listen, it's not cool. None of it was cool. I'm really sorry I made you go to the gym, of all places," he says.

To which I proudly reply, "I, actually I went to the gym of my own accord, I'll have you know."

"Yeah but, you're the guy that walks in PE and runs a seventeen-minute mile only it's actually three-quarters of a mile, but we have to quit because the bell is going to ring and you need time to change your clothes[103]," he says.

"Okay, that's a LOT of unnecessary detail," I say. "Anyway, I can't verify the time of my mile. I'd have to check the gradebook. I'm pretty sure I got an A."

"Everyone who gets dressed gets an A. Just like everyone gets a trophy or a blue ribbon, or whatever. Anyway, everyone gets an A."

---

[103] This is actually a highly recommended technique. No one can fault you for moving, no matter how slow. This is a good life philosophy. Be the turtle.

114

"Rude. Also, I've never been given a trophy and now I'm even more sad," I reply, admittedly, pathetically.

"Anyway," he says, "I need you to know that I'm truly sorry. It's just, things at home are a nightmare. My parents aren't handling any of this well. (We knew they wouldn't, of course.) Get this, my dad wants me to speak to the church about it. Confess my sins. I don't know."

"Do it."

"I know, crazy, right? I could never, wait, what?"

"I think you should totally do it. Except, not as a confession."

"Then what, exactly?" He says, confused.
"I don't know," I admit. "Get up there and just tell everyone who you are. Look, it's like, forty-seven people. And they're all old and mostly hard of hearing. It should be okay. You have to do it, anyway. So, embrace it, somehow."

"Embrace the fact that I'm about to stand up and say hallelujah, I'm a homosexual," he says.

"That's MAGNIFICENT alliteration."

"It could be a musicale."

"I'll start writing it now," I say.

"By the way, I talked to Mrs. S. Seriously, I just went in to apologize. I don't know why she... I mean, she didn't have to..." Tim states, out of nowhere.

"What did she do?"

"Oh, I figured you knew. Aren't you doing the program?" He asks.

"Yeah. I'm still doing it. I haven't seen her latest edits. Pages and pages of edits. I'm sure I still have a few hours left of work, at least." I urge him to get to the heart of the matter. "Anyway, WHAT? Are you working on the show? Did she have pity on you and say you could work a spot?"

"Um, well, she made me audition. She. She asked me to audition, that is."

"Oh my gosh! GET TO THE POINT. What are you? Who are you?"

And, I would be screaming except this is a telephone conversation and I'm in my house, and it's not late[104], per se, but, my parents would wonder. They're used to a certain, how shall we say, natural projection and excellent diction, but still.

I have manners.

"The audition went well," he says.

"Okay, I can see you're going to draw this out. Well, tell me everything. What did you sing? Were you prepared?"

---

[104] It's 8:17 PM, Central Standard Time.

He replies, "No. I definitely wasn't. Okay, so I went in to apologize. She looked at me, and for real, before I could say anything, she stared; you know the stare. She put down the purple pen and she looked at me, and she said, you know, you belong up on that stage."

That's it.

"That's it?"

"No, I was just pausing. I wanted your reaction. Am I telling this well?" He says, clearly amused with himself.

"OH MY GOSH. No. Yes. No. Just, what is it already?"

"Okay, you're right. It's late[105]. It was just so bizarre. I said, sure, I'm sorry I missed it, I wanted to be there, I just, I'm having a bit of a hard year. Or at least, that was what I was in the process of saying when she said, sing this. She just, she shoved music at me and said, I've got the CD. No kidding. I sang from the show. And now I'm... I'm kind of a lead? I guess?"

That's it.

"WHAT?!?!? What is happening? No. I knew this would happen. I LOVE this. This. This is a GREAT story[106]. What happened to the other guy? Or are you double cast in a part that was previously not double cast? Whatever! It doesn't even matter. Congratulations, my guy. This is fabulous!"

"Ha. I mean, thank you. It's very strange," he replies.

---

[105] It is 8:19 PM, Central Standard Time.

[106] Admittedly, the dramatic pauses could use some work.

"I'm living for it."

"So, anyway, I'm sorry."

"Apology accepted. You're a leading man."

"Oh, and also," he begins.

"Yes?"

"Hallelujah, I'm a homosexual."

"You're a homosexual."

We say simultaneously.

And it will be.

It will be a great musicale.

It was the first time that he heard it.

He was in his bedroom.

It was late at night.

He had the Bible opened and he was reading nothing in particular; he was mostly staring into space, opening and closing his eyes, thinking and praying and believing and battling and wondering and hoping and longing.

I accept you just the way you are.

He heard,

I always have.

And he heard,

I always will.

Ahem.

"Take your time son."

"Um, yes, I'd like to thank my dad for giving me this opportunity to speak. He'd like me to tell you today about my, I guess a bit about myself. Well, I'm sure you already know. I'm up here to confess, I guess.

This is weird.

Anyway, I'd like to quote some scripture. We are in church. That seems like a good place to start."

There are some awkward chuckles here because no one actually knows what Tim is doing onstage. He doesn't preach. He doesn't speak. Maybe he's previewing the spring musicale? Clearly it's anybody's guess, and when it's anybody's guess, the silence is oft accompanied by awkward laughing or throat clearing or nose blowing. Something to fill the void.

"Jesus says, No one comes to the father except through me in John chapter fourteen[107].

In the book of Romans, it says if you confess with your mouth and believe in your heart, you will be saved[108]. That's a paraphrase of course. There are ellipses on my paper to indicate as much, but... Anyway.

In Ephesians, it says, by grace and not your own doing you have been saved through faith[109]."

---

[107] John 14:6

[108] Romans 10:9

[109] Ephesians 2:8-9.

Amen.

Amen.

"Oh, thank you sir." So, this is going well.

"Our Bible says, over and over, to love Jesus and love others[110].

That's what it says. That's the message we can all agree to.

But I'm up here to confess.

I guess, to say I'm gay."

Low murmurs here. Francine purses her lips, he's sure, and says mmmmmhmmmm just a little too loud, just like she knew the whole time.

"My family is hurt by this. My dad and mom have asked me to repent and attend counseling sessions for possible remedies, and I have attempted all of this time after time after time and here we are.

The Bible says women are to be silent in church in favor of their men[111].

The Bible says picking up sticks on a Sunday gets you brutally murdered on the spot[112].

---

[110] John 15:12-13, and, like, seriously, thirty or forty other places. Or so.

[111] 1 Timothy 2:12

[112] Numbers 15:32-36. Again.

The Bible says don't have slaves, but if you do, you know, treat them well[113]. Another paraphrase.

The Bible is a series of books written at a moment in time.

Maybe a moment where women were supposed to be silent even though that makes no sense.

Maybe a moment where slavery was just some kind of way of life or something even though, again, we all know things never should have been that way.

Maybe some kind of moment in time where you should leave the sticks where they lie.

I dunno.

I do know that I'm gay.

This is my confession.

And.

It's not an apology.

I can't apologize anymore.

I am probably too young to say it, but I am in love, at least as much as a guy my age can be.

---

[113] Ephesians 6:5-8.

I still love my family and I hope they can figure out a way to love me back. And, by the way, I still very much love Jesus and love the church too. And I have to believe there's a place for me here. Maybe you disagree, dad, and that'd be not, like, super great news for me, but there are other churches, and if eventually I have to find one, I have faith that I'll find a community that accepts me for who I am.

As Jesus has already done. And, frankly, as I wish you and mom would do."

Amen.

Amen.

He did it.

He really did it.

Of course, this is a story.

A story about two people.

It's probably made up. It's probably just a work of fiction. It can't be true that this would be cause for rejection.

He was a man of God.

And he was a man of God.

This is a story about two people in love with Jesus and in love with each other; two people who just happen to be two men, and that's it. That's the whole story.

Why does it still matter? Why does it still need to be told? Why is it still interesting? Why is it still debated? Why is it still a controversy?

They don't know. They're too busy loving life and loving each other. And laughing. They laugh a lot.

And that's more than enough.

"Mrs. Timoth?"

"Very funny, young man."

"He still calls you that."

Tim wasn't sure if he should, or should not, approach the parental units so soon after his PowerPoint-Free Presentation, or whatever that was. He wasn't sure what kind of damage he'd done to his family, their livelihood, or the church. His father barely comes home. But his mom, at least, seemed open to communication as indicated by the mildly humorous initial response.

"Oh?"

Then.

"I like Charlie, you know. He's got quite a vocabulary."

That threw him off, a little. He never expected his friend[114], as it were, to be liked. He also never expected to be thinking of themselves as friends, as they were, so soon. But that's what they were, were they not?

He smiles a little, at that.

"Yes, he does. Listen, mom, I, I'm sorry."

"Oh?"

Then.

"No."

---

[114] Quote, unquote.

"I'M sorry," she says. Too formally, too stoic, she says, "On behalf of your father and I, I am sorry. We've tried so hard, son. I don't know. I don't think we can ever be the parents you need."

"Mom."

Then.

"I'm proud of you."

This catches him off guard. He doesn't respond, doesn't know how.

"I think you said what you needed to say. I think you did what you needed to do. I think you're brave, you know. That's what you are. My son. So brave."

This is acceptance. Or, it isn't. He doesn't know why he's crying.

"Son, your father has a job to do. He's good at his job. He's a spiritual leader. And I'm his wife.

But I'm also your mother.

And. I love you. We, we love you. He loves you."

But his father isn't home.

"You should graduate high school and you should go off to college somewhere. And you should live your life. That's what you should do."

She's crying as she walks away.

He knows her as the solid foundation of his family, the unwavering, the unshakable, and he's never seen her cry before.

She turns.

"I will never stop loving you, son.

I don't know how."

The night of the show is upon us and, surprisingly, Tim's dad let him keep his part. And that's great for me because I'm thinking Mrs. S expected me to understudy, and let's all just breathe sighs of relief, collectively, that, for the benefit of all present, this didn't come to fruition.

And by all present, I mean several hundred people. This auditorium is full and the energy is abuzz! What a thrill!

That is, I'm thrilled. Tim does not seem thrilled. Sarah, she seems nervous but ever-poised as usual.

"Hey, are you excited about this? Opening night and whatnot! Huzzah!"

(Nobody actually says huzzah.)

"My parents aren't coming. They said they didn't care what I did. Well, she. My dad just hasn't even really been home. He'll come home for food and change his clothes but he's always in meetings, at church, blah blah blah. It's so obvious he's ignoring me. And he's trying to save his reputation, his livelihood, everything I've screwed up. But, I mean, of course he cares, they care. She just kind of said I could do whatever I wanted, that I was old enough, and that I should start looking at what I was going to do after high school. Essentially like they weren't kicking me out but saying, 'just get out as soon as you can, son.'

Oh. She also made sure she was quite clear in saying that she was proud of me. That was weird."

"Oh. Wow."

"Yeah, and, get this, they don't want me to come to church anymore. You either. She actually told me to see if I could get you to stop coming. She started mentioning other churches. You know. Which is actually her being helpful, I think. But, yeah, you said it best, I guess. Wow, right?"

I offer, "Listen, tonight you've only got one thing to worry about. It's the beauty and drama of the theatre, right?"

"A few nights ago, I actually felt like I heard God." Tim says. "I know, super cheesy[115], yeah? Maybe I didn't. But it felt like it, you know. He or she or they or whoever, this voice, it really stood out. I know it's weird, but I heard someone very prominent say,"

"I accept you?" I finish.

"Whoa." He says.

"I always have?" I add.

"Exactly. Yes. Exactly that."

Through tears, I say, "I always will. You know what I think? I think we both heard what we needed to hear when we needed to hear it."

"I can't believe, I mean that's basically word-for-word," he says. "Okay, so I want to say something dumb, but it's just that, I kind of almost maybe more than like you."

---

[115] It is well established by now that I *live* for cheese.

"Ew, yeah, that's dumb. But also, I'm crying, so you get what you get. Why don't you just go out there and have a good show and we can talk about all of this dumb stuff some more later?"

"Okay."

"Break a leg. Sarah, you too. You, of course, who were present for this entire conversation but heard absolutely nothing."

She says, "Of course. I mean, what? You're both dumb. That's about the entirety of what I heard, I'm certain."

With that, they're off to places.

I go to find the crackers[116].

---

[116] This is super bad for your singing voice, I think. Yeah, don't eat crackers or dairy, probably not cookies before singing. Oh and never eat in costume. Costumers everywhere will thank me for this. To them, I will say, I hope you paid $12.95 for this. If so, you're welcome.

By the way, I thrive in the chorus.

I'm, like, really good at it. For example, my first stage direction is to cross downstage left to upstage right. There's a fountain in the middle, and I'm supposed to linger a bit there, you know, so my cross lasts for two and a half pages and it looks like the street is busy even though it is, in fact, the same three or four people over and over again. This is heavy, Shakespearean stuff. And I just feel like a lot of people struggle to sell these sorts of crosses. You know, we have some students who will, I don't know, inexplicably examine the fountain as if it's some extreme curiosity, or perhaps they're some sort of inspector or detective combing for fingerprints. Hokey. Honestly, who but their parents is buying that[117]? Me, on the other hand, my casual saunter is so real, it's as if I walk this street every day. My pause at the fountain is so natural, I know my mother is staring at me, loving this, beaming with pride, she doesn't even care about the arguably-much-more-important dialogue happening downstage. That's acting. And she knows it.

I am thriving.

---

[117] Their parents aren't buying it either. They already brought the flowers and, honey, you're getting them anyway.

Crackers, it turns out, might be terrible fodder for singers[118]. I have, sort of, crumbs in my mouth and they're, kind of, spewing forth during this number. Hitting other chorus members. Saltined saliva. Just a bit. Whatever. My dancing makes up for it. And I finish my cross.

I only have a few scenes, of course, but I'm nailing them. Otherwise I spend my time waiting in the wings, eyes and ears on Tim and Sarah. Mostly on Tim. He's such a gift to our theatre program, and even with such limited preparation, this role really fits him.

I'm excited because my next stage direction is to walk by with two suitcases and hand one to him, tip my hat, and I'm off. It's another nearly full cast scene, and I added the handoff of the suitcase myself because I wanted some interaction with our leading man. My leading man. Otherwise we're not blocked together at all, which was some kind of oversight, and, honestly, he had to get his prop from somewhere. Mrs. S either didn't notice or did. In any case, the hat tip, again, completely natural, was all hers.

Genius.

I am rocking this fedora.

---

[118] See! I told you so!

The thing about props, suitcases, really any container, the thing that sets me apart, is I'm always thinking about the contents, how much they should weigh. This is because it drives me crazy how actors, real ones, people on television and the movies stand there with a cup of coffee so unbearably, obviously empty. I guess I get it. I suppose I sympathize with the idea of not wanting to get burned or spilling or something. Maybe the prop budget is too small for coffee-like contents. I don't know. I doubt it. But honestly, sir, you're Ben Affleck. You've got, like, two hundred and seven Oscars[119] or whatever. Maybe you don't, who cares[120], just, the point is, act like the cup is full. It's literally your job. And how hard is it? How am I supposed to believe you're Batman or some kind of astronaut or athlete or you even ever actually liked Jennifer Garner when you can't even fake sloshing around some kind, any kind, of liquid?

So it goes without saying that I've spent a lot of time analyzing these pieces of luggage, how I would carry them if they had anything in them. Tim's - the one I hand him - I've decided contains six folded up t-shirts and three beautiful, cable knit sweaters, and four pairs of pants, at least one of which I hope is purple as I'm handing it off.

---

[119] Two Academy Awards, two British Academy Film Awards, three Golden Globe Awards, one Director's Guild, one Producer's Guild, and two Screen Actor's Guild Awards. And three more dollars for Wikipedia.

[120] He doesn't. I care. See note.

He leans in.

It's as if he has to whisper something to me, only to me, and he puts his face upstage of mine even though he's a central role, the focal point to my passerby, and what could he possibly have to say only, unbelievably and very, very quickly, perhaps imperceptibly to everyone but me, only me, obviously me?

He kisses me on the cheek.

And walks away to continue the scene with his empty suitcase in hand.

I walk off.

He kissed me[121].

So, it doesn't matter that he sucked at carrying his suitcase. That it's obviously empty. That the whole auditorium, including my mother, knows it's empty[122].

He kissed me.

We talked about the suitcase, you know. Of course we did. Of course, while he's trying to memorize countless lines and songs, I tell him how important it is to believe in the weight of the suitcase. Really lift the thing, carry it, struggle, play it up. It matters.

It doesn't matter.

I guess.

Only, okay, obviously I can't leave it at that; it does. It totally does, it definitely matters. It just matters so much less because two weeks ago we were fighting about holding hands in public and now, in front of everyone, everyone and no one, no one but me and God, I have had my first kiss.

So what if the guy sucks at handling his props?

He kissed me.

---

121 So *not* ew.

122 She already brought him flowers too.

I am thriving.

TIM/ Tell me more of your favorite words.

CHARLIE/ Kilig.

TIM/ Weird. I like it. Is it Scandinavian or Klingon or something?

CHARLIE/ Tagalog, actually.

TIM/ I am pretty sure those are delicious, delicious Girl Scout cookies.

CHARLIE/ Not tagalong. Tagalog. But, you're right. Delicious. Anyway, Kilig is, it's butterflies in your stomach, I think. Something like that. Oh, and I was liking this word, saudade, but now forelsket is definitely more my speed. It's Norwegian for the euphoric feeling of falling in love.

TIM/ Ew.

CHARLIE/ Kummerspeck.

TIM/ Dirty. I hate.

CHARLIE/ Technically a negative word, but still very much a fave.

TIM/ Wait. Is it dirty?

CHARLIE/ Nah. Bacon grief.

TIM/ Pardon?

CHARLIE/ I think, more literally, grief bacon. Something about emotional overeating. You know, like maybe after a breakup someone eats a pint of ice cream, or, in this case, a pound of bacon. It's German.

TIM/ Have you ever eaten a pound of bacon?

CHARLIE/ Well, to be the most fair, I'm not really one to weigh my bacon. Also, I understand it shrinks when you cook it[123], so maybe I have consumed what was once a pound of bacon, but in its previous, uncooked state. Also, I'm elated to report that it would not take a breakup or, really, any particular sorrow for me to participate in any such mass-consumption of bacon. Bacon is delicious. Participating in its delicious, delicious consumption needn't require any particular state of emotion. For me. In reality, I'm getting a little emotional right now.

TIM/ Me too.

CHARLIE/ Tearing up as we type.

---

[123] It shrinks because the fat melts away when cooked. Some disappointed posters report bacon shrinkage of up to 43%!

Let's go!

Okay, but have you checked your windshield washing fluid levels?

Too soon?

We pull up to this building, fairly non-descript. There is a rainbow flag[124] outside. You don't see a whole lot of that around here. It does a little to calm the nerves, but not much. Otherwise, some things that one can immediately take note of include too many flower beds and seven out of ten cars in the parking lot with those equal sign bumper stickers[125]. And a cross[126].

So, this is probably the right place.

I can count the number of times I've visited other churches on one hand.

This is Tim's first time going to not-his-father's congregation.

So, yes, nervous is a good word. See also anxious, tense, on edge.

Tim grabs my hand.

This is still new.

---

[124] First displayed in 1978 in San Francisco, created by Gilbert Baker.

[125] From the Human Rights Campaign. You can accidentally get them for free but it's nice to donate a dollar or three, in tandem with our Wikipedia contributions! Every little bit counts.

[126] Available at Cracker Barrel's nationwide.

And interesting.

And exciting.

Cool.

It does calm the nerves, a bit. Knowing that we're here, together. To see what "affirming" really means.

Tim looks at me.

I look at him.

He does this weird sort of nod thing. What does that mean? Yes? Yes, what? I have no idea, but of course I nod back like it's a cultural thing. A norm or something. To nod as if answering an invisible question or further acknowledging one's presence in this place as if either of these are necessary. They aren't.

Anyway.

We go inside.

The service was interesting.

One hundred and twelve people. I counted. I do that sort of thing.

That's not to say I didn't pay attention.

I did. I do. Kind of.

The pastor's sermon was fairly ordinary, or it started that way. Then, all of the sudden, he introduced his sexuality and spoke about different understandings of the Bible, specifically wherein homosexuality is mentioned in modern translations. Something about seven verses[127] and all of them being, for the most part, taken out of context and without proper understanding.

Seven verses? I wondered if that was really all because, when you're gay and someone wants you to be other-than, it's actually all you hear about and you'd think there were, more like, three thousand seven hundred and forty-six verses and all of them explicitly state THOU SHALT NOT BE GAY LEST THOU SHALT WANT TO BE DAMNED TO ETERNAL HELLFIRE.

(They don't.)

This pastor, he said, did you know the Bible mentions money more than two thousand times[128]? Then he said, the offering plates are in the lobby on your way out.

He's funny. This one.

---

[127] Not referenced here on purpose.

[128] There are, according to one source, 2,350 verses about money.

The songs were similar to the songs we sing in youth group, so, clearly, this is a Contemporary Christian service. There was this strange part of the service where you're obligated to meet people and to talk to them and it seemed to go on FOREVER[129] and, really, what do you say other than hi, nice to meet you, great hair, and God be with you?

Eventually Tim and I were just standing in our pew, talking to ourselves, which was fine. He asked me for a favorite word. I said Mamihlapinatapai[130]. He said I made that up. I said I didn't. Then I said, God be with you and he said also with you and we sat down.

After the service, people form a line in the center aisle to exit. The pastor greets people on the way out, seems to be hugging everyone.

It feels funereal. Or something. I'm not sure, but here we are in line.

"Hi!"

That's the pastor's line when we finally make our way to the front. We took a number and are seventy-fourth and seventy-fifth in line. This is what it feels like, but here we are.

"Hi. Um, I'm Charles."

I never refer to myself as Charles.

---

[129] Seven and a half minutes. I timed it.

[130] "To look at each other, hoping that either will offer to do something, which both parties much desire done but are unwilling to do."

I'm nervous.

"This is Timoth. Uh, Timothy."

"Hi!"

The pastor repeats. Then,

"This is your first time here?"

It's a question, but also he obviously knows this is our first time here.

"Yeah. Um, yes."

I say.

So, this is going well.

"Well. Welcome. We're very glad you're here."

He says some other things, and then he says,

"How long have you two been dating?"

Several things are weird about this, chief among them are that we are obviously boyfriends and we are obviously at a church and this is something we can do without shame or fear and maybe, just maybe, this can be something that, for a while, sure, we are proud of and excited about, but then, mostly, for me, for us, maybe it can just be.

Normal.

And so in three days it will have been six months since an algorithm introduced us and in three days after that it will have been six months since we first met and six months since we first went to three restaurants in one night and then in three days after that it will be six months since you first left me to go on your family vacation and six months since I thought, well, that was nice, weird but nice, and eight days after that it will have been six months since your first of many returns and our first of many presents, because I love presents and presents are super important and you can feel free to still and forever bring me all the presents all the time and, anyway, the day after that I told you I thought I loved you and the present probably helped and either way it was probably premature but either way I was right. I loved you. And six months later I love you. And six months after that it will be a year because I'm grand at mathematics, see, and I did that all in my head, see, and when we graduate you probably should buy me a really good present like I'm kind of in the market for these new pants or maybe...

Author's Note

The author thinks it is important to note that a great many of the weird or interesting or amusing words in this novel came from one fantastic article.

There are many search results when considering obscure words for love, romance, and the like. The one that includes the title word which began the author's journey down the rabbit's hole, as they say, is from "the world's leading business media brand" (whatever that means), *Fast Company*. The title of the article is *"'Grief Bacon' and 12 other untranslatable words about love."*

Isn't that fun?

It was first published June 13, 2016.

Acknowledgements

I had the best time writing this book and it wouldn't be NEARLY the thing that it is without the help of a lot of humans! Thank you so much to the following people for reading parts or all of this and providing invaluable feedback along the way: dad, sister, husband, *Chelsea Cain & The Q's,* and my friends. Special thanks to Mindy LaHood and Mary Aylmer for early edits and to Annie Hicks for the late edits. Thanks to Kate Klise for coaching me along the way! And, of course, an extra special thank you to Paige for the beautiful cover and interior hearts!

It might or might not be obvious, but I've never written a book before. I've always wanted to. I just was always stuck on the fact that I wanted to make sure I said just the right things to just the right people at just the right time. That's probably dumb, though. If it isn't, heck, even if it is, I hope I've done something somewhat close to that with *bacon grief.* I sincerely hope this little book finds the way to those that need it.

I hope you find some comfort in knowing that you are loved just the way you are.

This is a work of fiction. I don't even eat bacon.

I wish I were kidding. I'm not. I know. I know. I'm missing out.

Though it is a work of fiction, much of it is my experience. I know Christianity can be a rough upbringing for a lot of LGBTQIA+ youth.

I don't think it has to be. My prayer is that you find your people. And that you never change.

About the Author

Joel Shoemaker has been a librarian for a decade and a magician for three!

He lives in central Illinois with his husband, and dog, Maximus. He consumes an inordinate amount of cheese. *bacon grief* is his debut novel.